Pullers

10/23/98

To
Becky Argall:
Thanks for all your help
and support during the last
three years. I can't tell
you how much it all
meant.

Gratefully
inscribed,

Tom

Pullers

A Novel

By Tom Graves

HASTINGS HOUSE
Norwalk, Connecticut

This book is a work of fiction. Names, characters, places, and incidents either are products of the author's imagination or are used fictitiously. Any resemblance to actual events or locales or persons, living or dead, is entirely coincidental.

Hastings House
50 Washington Street
Norwalk, CT 06854

Library of Congress Catalogin-in-Publication Data is available

ISBN: 0-8038-9424-4

Manufactured in the United States of America

10 9 8 7 6 5 4 3 2 1

For Denise

Author's Note

Arm wrestling is a real sport, a sport where men of almost inhuman strength routinely risk breaking one another's arms for the glory of winning and prize money that barely covers expenses. The pros, those who participate in organized tournaments, refer to these matches as "pulls" and to each other as "pullers." Generally speaking, pullers shun the barroom matches we have all seen in movies—unless, of course, they happen to run short on cash.

Unlike the most well-known literary depiction of arm wrestling—in Hemingway's *The Old Man and the Sea*, where two characters arm wrestle to a standstill that lasts for days—a long pull in a tournament might last ten seconds. Two or three seconds would be the norm. It's fast, it's furious, and if something goes wrong, somebody gets hurt.

Pulling, like any sport, is a world unto itself. What I have attempted in this novel is to present that world. It will be up to the pullers themselves to tell me whether I have succeeded.

—*Tom Graves*

"Wild is a category of its own."

—Larry Brown

Pullers

Chapter 1

Cockroaches. Nice American cockroaches. *Periplaneta americana*. The size about, oh, as long as the first two joints of your little finger. A whole boiling swarm of them.

Like everyone else, Carroll Thurston had hated cockroaches his whole life. Which was the whole point. They made his skin crawl every time he caught sight of one.

But not now.

He'd learned to love them. And it wasn't easy to love a cockroach. But now he did, every goddamn one of 'em. He'd had to. Otherwise he couldn't do what it was he did.

These weren't just any cockroaches. They were *mail-order* cockroaches. Grown and bred in a sterile laboratory by people wearing white lab coats. Of course he could have gone to any run-down part of Memphis—any one of Memphis's housing projects would do—and gotten all he needed for free. But the fact was you never knew where homegrown roaches had been. No telling what kind of germs and all they carried.

No, Carroll Thurston wanted *clean* roaches, roaches with a pedigree. Roaches a man could trust.

Carroll kept his roaches in a ten-gallon aquarium filled with shreds of corrugated cardboard. Because cockroaches are the Houdinis of the insect kingdom, he took the extra precaution of placing a heavy Plexiglas lid on top.

He'd learned an awful lot about roaches in the last year. For example, they were basically unchanged despite millions of years of evolution. They could also survive a nuclear war better than just about any other living organism. And people just hated the shit out of them. Would rather die than touch one.

Carroll had read that a fear of cockroaches was a learned behavior. Kids over the age of four picked up the fear from their parents and peers. Researchers had gone so far as to put fake roaches in the drinking glasses of kids under four years old. They had no problem at all drinking their water with a roach staring up at them from the bottom of the glass. The dread came later.

Smiling to himself at how grown men would run at the sight of a cockroach, Carroll Thurston tilted the lid off the aquarium, reached in, and grabbed a seething fistful of roaches. Without a grunt or a grimace he quickly stuffed the whole squirming mass into his mouth and crunched down hard three...four...five times.

"Hmmm, kind of like popcorn shrimp," he thought to himself as he washed it all down with a big slug of Diet Coke.

Chapter 2

Near rock-bottom of those annual lists that rate cities according to their desirability (or lack thereof) is the sleepy town of Pine Bluff, Arkansas, an old railroad and paper mill community that still seems stuck in the belly of the Great Depression. The city's most famous resident had been Martha Mitchell, the loudmouthed wife of Watergate alumnus and former Attorney General John Mitchell. Elvis Presley, natives are quick to tell you, performed at the Pine Bluff Coliseum once during his tours in the seventies.

Other than a few stoplights and strip malls, the town hadn't taken on a lot of luster since the World War—the first one.

Although Pine Bluff is, and always has been, a God-fearing town, the nineties are the nineties and good ole boys will be good ole boys. Bad Bill's Hawg Trawf (the Trawf for short) is the place where they generally went to do it. Bad Bill lived up to his nickname by charging patrons a one-time membership fee of twenty dollars, which stiffed all the out-of-towners, who in all likelihood would never come back, while giving the locals a place to water, dance, and raise hell without paying a nightly cover charge.

The Trawf was a metal building that covered five acres and looked like one of those enormous sheds used to house combines and cotton pickers. A crude cartoon of cowboys lined up at a slop trough to drink beer suds served as the invitation to all passers-by from the sides of the building. Bad Bill had a tidy cottage industry on the side selling t-shirts, ball caps, mugs, and you name it emblazoned with the cartoon and his logo. A Bad Bill's T-shirt immediately notified one's Pine Bluff neighbor on which side of the Christian equation you stood.

At the Trawf, beer was sold in Mason jars at a dollar-fifty a pop. There were four pool tables, a shuffleboard, two video poker machines, a backgammon table (which went unused), a stage for the bands, a broken mechanical bull in the corner, and a stout hardwood table used for arm wrestling. In the ten years the Trawf had been in business—since liquor by the drink finally passed during a local referendum—arm wrestling had become a surprisingly popular form of entertainment. On Friday nights Bill held an arm wrestling tournament with the winner collecting two hundred fifty dollars in prize money. Farm boys from a ten-county area came to try their hand (and arm) at the sport, and Bill made a sweet profit charging each newcomer a membership fee plus a twenty-dollar entry for the tournament. Of course, the prize money was a small part of the action. The winner could, if he placed his bets at the proper odds, snag another four or five hundred dollars, better than two weeks' take-home pay.

The tournament was closely followed by the locals who shouted out bets throughout matches. The action often became so heated that fistfights erupted among the spectators, mostly over drunken accusations of cheating. Bad Bill and his beefy bouncers made sure no one welshed on bets. But he could not have cared less if some of the boys wanted to take their arguments out to the parking lot.

Pine Bluff's undisputed arm wrestling champion was

Sampson Jackson, a local rowdy who ran a car battery shop. Sampson seldom had an off night at the wrestling table, but that never stopped locals from trying to best him or from showing off for their girlfriends how long they could last. Unless he was beered up or in a particularly foul mood, Sampson Jackson usually tried to make the other guy come off looking good. After all, it kept them coming back.

And it kept his name out there to attract fresh meat from out of town. Some guys drove all the way from Memphis to give him a go. They always lost.

This particular Friday night Sampson Jackson had had his fill of beer and then some. Although a few of the boys had made him break a sweat, he had beat them handily, slamming his opponents' knuckles as hard as possible into the table. Any kind of macho antics made the crowd hoot and yeehaw with all their heart, and Sampson Jackson was not above playing to the hometown regulars.

"Well I'll be a three-balled billygoat," one of the hometown boys said as he pointed towards the entrance. "Take a gander at what just come through the front door."

The two men who were paying their one-time membership fees at the entrance made several at the bar shake their heads to make sure they weren't seeing things. The bigger man looked like the handiwork of a Gold's Gym. He stood six-feet-four inches or so and had a twenty-inch neck with arms that seemed even bigger. He towered over the smaller man, who stood about five-five and was pinch-ass skinny. The small one was completely bald on top with hair growing from the temples that draped down to his shoulders. His black, deep-set eyes gave him a don't-fuck-with-me appearance, like an Arab getting ready to gut an enemy. The larger man sported a spiky crew cut and a close-cropped beard. Both men wore identical t-shirts that read WE'RE QUEER DEAR.

But what drew every eye in Bad Bill's tavern to the odd couple was the chain the big one held like a leash that disappeared down the front of the smaller man's pants.

"Is he leading that fucker by the dick?" Sampson asked to no one in particular.

"Look like a couple of tailgaters on the prowl," another answered.

"Bad Bill ought to monkey-jump their faggot asses right out of here," said the fellow who had just gotten beat at the arm wrestling table.

"Naw, he's too interested in making a dime or two off 'em. He wouldn't run off a couple of fudge-packing eight-balls like those two. Hell, he let you boys in, didn't he?"

"I wonder what the hell they're doing here in Pine Bluff in the first place. We keep the taxidermists busy enough as it is."

The big man, with his partner close at heel, strolled over to the arm wrestling table and with a wide grin extended a huge right hand.

"Hi there. I'm Scud Matthews and this is my best boy, Itch. I know you folks ain't too accustomed to our kind here in Arkansas, but you know the New Orleans gay community has some pretty bad ass arm wrestlers. I've heard a lot about you. You *are* Sampson Jackson?"

"Yeah, that's my name all right," Sampson answered in a wary, patronizing tone as he reluctantly proffered his hand. But, he had to admit, he *was* flattered. They had heard of him all the way down to New Orleans! It did bother him that the queer community knew about him though. He didn't want anybody in Pine Bluff thinking he had gone funny.

"So what brings you girls here to Bad Bill's?"

Scud narrowed his eyes and his grin hardened. "I thought we might do us a little arm rasslin'."

"From the looks of things, I thought you boys might be more interested in playing round-eye than arm wrestling."

Scud Matthews's eyebrows forked together.

"Hell, I thought you were serious about this game. I've come all the way from New Orleans and I've got five hundred dollars that says I can whip your redneck ass. But if all you're interested in is swapping bullshit…"

"Five hundred you say? Okay coach, you're on…provided you wash your hands first. I don't want to be catching any fag cooties or anything. And I want to see the five hundred first."

Itch reached in the back pocket of his drooping Levi's and peeled off five Ben Franklins from a fist-sized wad of bills.

"All right, Hercules, now let's see *your* five hundred."

"The name's Sampson, gents. Bad Bill will vouch for me."

Bill solemnly nodded agreement.

"Then that's settled," said Scud. "Just one more thing. I don't want no pussy-eating sonofabitch's cooties getting on me. You wash your hands too."

"It's a deal. Let's shake on it."

Sampson stuck out a hand and laughed and Scud Matthews, with a grin slowly working over his face, clasped it in a firm, manly handshake.

"Okay boys, it's time for the rubber to meet the road," said Sampson. "Bill, you hold the money and do the refereeing. Pull up a chair, Scud. It's clobberin' time. Oh, one more thing. Why have you got your little partner there on that leash?"

"So he doesn't get loose and kill anybody."

Sampson Jackson one-eyed his opponent as the two men faced off on opposite sides of the table, their elbows resting on the table top and forearms sticking straight up in the air.

"Okay fellows, get yourself a good grip," Bad Bill instructed them.

Both men carefully entwined their hands, making sure the grip was exact and without weakness. After a minute or so of adjustments, Bill looked at them and asked if they were ready.

"Ready."

"Ready."

Bill put his hands on top of theirs for a second, commanded "go," and withdrew them quickly.

Sampson Jackson had wrestled dozens of pumped-up Arnolds like this one before. Bodybuilders were easy money. They were seldom as strong as they looked and Sampson had the added advantage of not having bulging biceps. Although both his arms were solid as marble, no one could tell that. Especially with his arms covered by long-sleeved flannel shirts. He had used his natural strength to his advantage even in the Marines. He won every drink during his whole hitch. This fag would go down easy.

Only thing is, he wasn't. This guy was a lot stronger than Sampson would have guessed and was stone steady. Their fingertips had already begun to turn a deep shade of blue, but their arms had barely budged, still locked at a perfect 90 degree angle from the table. Both men had begun to sweat through their clothes, and beads of sweat stung their eyes as they rolled from their foreheads into their faces.

Scud Matthews showed subtle signs of tiring and began rapid breathing exercises. Sampson was no doubt beginning to grind his opponent down and he felt his arm begin to take control, inching forward, gaining ground. He wasn't going to slam any knuckles, but he had him and they both knew it. The betting among spectators had increased to fever pitch.

Only inches away from defeat, Scud Matthews began to recite a mantra that to the crowd sounded like "oh-yum-yum."

"Oh-yum-yum, oh-yum-yum, oh-yum-yum, oh-yum-yum," and Scud began to rally, almost miraculously. Sampson could not believe he was being pushed backwards.

When they had reached the 90 degree position again, Scud Matthews seemed to falter and Sampson quickly forced his arm to almost a hair's breadth of the table. Scud began to recite his mantra in double-time, "oh-yum-yum, oh-yum-yum, oh-yum-yum, oh-yum-yum," faster and faster until he began to regain position. In an unbelievable burst of strength, Scud Matthews had reversed their positions with Sampson's knuckles a fraction from the table. Sampson, in utter panic, bellowed like a bull with a brand at its hide. He grit his teeth so hard they seemed in danger of cracking to pieces.

Sampson's arm moved forward slightly and then crumpled. It was all over. He had been beaten. The crowd was in shock and soundless.

Both men glared at each other for what seemed several minutes, gasping for air. Finally, Scud Matthews wheezed, "I guess...I'll take...that five hundred...and the prize money."

"I guess...you won't...you cheatin' fag...I wouldn't...give you...the sweat off my..."

"Fuck *you* asshole...I won...fair and...square."

Bad Bill handed Scud his two-hundred fifty dollars in prize money. "Like he said, Sampson, he won fair and square. Pay off your bet."

Sampson reached into his boot and pulled out a small .22 caliber pistol. The crowd parted like Moses' waters.

"Put it down, Sampson. You're gonna wind up in jail or the electric chair if you do something stupid," Bill coached him in a calm, fatherly voice.

"Tell you what I'll do," Scud hesitantly began, his eyes focused on the barrel of Sampson's small pistol. "I'll wrestle you again. You win, I pay you the five hundred dollars. I win, you owe me the five hundred and not a penny more. I don't want anybody saying I cheated, even if we all know I won fair and square. Let's settle things here and now. My five hundred still says I can kick your ass."

Sampson smiled an ugly little smile. "Fine with me sissy boy. We'll see how lucky you are a second time. Here, Bill, take this before I get really pissed off." He slid the pistol over to Bill.

"This time I want to see *your* money on the table," Scud said, thumping the table for emphasis. Bill and Sampson pooled the money together and left it at the end of the table. Scud did the same at the opposite end.

Towels were brought and they wiped down and squared off across the wrestling table. Bill gave the command to go and both arms tensed at the ninety degree position. Scud began to move his arm forward quickly, then let Sampson push him back. He did this in a toying fashion, chuckling to himself.

"You know, you really shouldn't welsh on bets. Now I've got to collect a little interest."

Through gritted teeth Sampson hissed, "Fuck you, cocksucker."

"No, Hercules, you're the one who's fucked."

With a lightning move, Scud bowed Sampson's wrist backwards until it nearly touched the hair on the back of his arm and began to bear down hard. In the space of one or two seconds, Sampson let out a high scream that brought Bad Bill's entire five acres to a standstill. A slow, wet cracking sound, like green wood being splintered grain-by-grain, was heard by all the spectators.

Sampson's scream abruptly stopped and, like a catfish out of water, he swallowed air for one long pause. His tongue then lolled out of his mouth and his face fell hard into the hardwood table.

Enraged, Bad Bill and his bouncers encircled Scud Matthews while he casually collected his winnings. As they did, Itch began to slowly pull the chain out from the front of his pants, which was attached to a special bore .38 revolver, customized to make maximum noise. Pointing it in the air, he pulled the trigger twice with two ear-shattering reports that rolled around inside the immense metal building like waves from a cannon blast. At least one hundred cowboy hats dove for the floor.

Scud and Itch calmly walked to the door and Scud turned and blew a kiss to the frozen faces.

"Stay smoochy, boys."

They skidded out of the parking lot sending rooster tails of pea gravel onto the gleaming Turtle Waxed surfaces of the rows of pickup trucks.

Chapter 3

To a one, all they were after was a power fuck. The truth was, they got off on being pounded in bed like ground chuck and smothered in arms strong enough to snap their spines like a baby bird's. Carroll Thurston aimed to please. If a pounding is what they wanted, a pounding is what they got. To them he was simply a dick with a smile and huge forearms at the end of it. For nothing extra, he'd throw in the promise of true love...if they wanted it.

Being the world's second-ranked super heavyweight arm wrestler had its good points and its bad. Women regarded him as an irresistible sexual freak, and he saw nothing particularly bad in that. After all, he had a warm bed waiting any time he needed one. And pounding them was a lot better than pounding the alternative.

It never failed that dainty, bird-like women, usually around five-one or -two and tipping the scales at roughly one hundred pounds, couldn't keep their hands off him. They wanted to know what physical power *felt* like. With Carroll's physique shaped like an inverted triangle, they were all too eager to scoot under his six-five, three hundred-pound frame to have a little piece of that power ground into them. Carroll couldn't remember the last time he had kissed a woman during sex. But he had kissed a damn sight more headboards than he would care to remember.

Not that Carroll was complaining. Just once, though, he'd like to hook up with some strapping big-boned gal who wanted to power fuck *him*. And a little intelligent conversation would go a long way. Maybe find one who had ever read a book. Or spent a semester or two in college.

Take Heather Madison, for instance. When she found out her Memphis bartender was famous for more than his margaritas, she began what Carroll referred to as the bird dance. It usually started with being peppered by questions about arm wrestling and the size of his arms, which he had to admit few could keep their eyes off. It wasn't every day you saw someone with twenty-inch forearms. Arms that big literally stopped traffic. It wasn't uncommon for drivers to come to a screeching halt to gape at his arms. In Japan, Carroll had caused major traffic snarls just walking down the street taking in the sights. He joked that they thought Godzilla was on the loose.

After a few drinks (Carroll usually watered them down to see how much acting they were willing to do) they managed to find a way to touch him, to pet his arms.

"Want to wrestle me, hon?" they would get around to asking with a giggle and a blush.

"Your place or mine, sweetheart?" was his corny canned reply. It usually did the trick. It got him into Heather's apartment.

Heather was the type who liked giving orders. "You get on bottom and I'll get on top," she instructed as she sat astraddle of him. "Mmm. Now hold me around the waist. No, tighter. Tighter. Now lift me up and down. That's it. *Oh yeah.*"

He moved in and out of her like a short-stroked piston.

After twenty or thirty minutes of intensely aerobic lovemaking, they were both bathed in sweat. Women were invariably disappointed if they weren't.

Heather slipped out of bed, kissed him softly on the lips, and returned a few minutes later carrying a warm towel for Carroll and two cans of Gatorade. In her own petite way, Heather was strikingly pretty. She was a hairdresser at a snotty Memphis salon called Prix de Beauté, and like all hairdressers she was studiedly into chic, sporting an ink-black Louise Brooks hair bob with matching black clothes all the way down to her tiny black panties.

Carroll picked up the panties and twirled them a second or two around his index finger. Heather, who was balled up next to him in a post-coital silence, suppressed a small giggle. On impulse Carroll brought the crotch to his nose and sniffed. It was Heather all right. She slapped his arm and said in half-hearted indignation, "*Car*-roll!"

"I love the way you smell."

She managed a small smile. "Did I rate high enough for you to want them as a souvenir?"

"Sure." Carroll was surprised that he wasn't lying.

Heather fixed him with a sober stare. "Was this just another one-nighter, Carroll?"

"Most women consider one time enough," he replied. "They've bagged their arm wrestler and go on to another trophy."

"I'm not like that," she spat back, fire in her eyes.

"Maybe not. You kissed me."

"Of course I kissed you."

"Well, you're the first who's really bothered to kiss me in three or four months. And I wasn't celibate."

"Sounds to me like you've been chasing the wrong women."

"Could be."

Chapter 4

Monday nights were nothing but a bunch of drunk pricks playing grab-ass in the guise of watching Monday night football as far as Carroll was concerned. The Bombay, where Carroll tended bar, was normally an upscale café well-situated in Memphis's small Overton Square nightclub district. Happy hour drew an eclectic mix of lawyers, hospital workers, and midtown bohemians who regarded The Bombay Bar as the only watering hole that mattered. For local color, it was certainly the most entertaining place to be. Monday nights, however, were a riot of loudmouths and lowlifes swilling pitchers of beer, eating mountains of free hors d'oeuvres, and screaming their lungs out while watching the big-screen projector TV.

Carroll did not find team spirit contagious. Monday nights for him meant tossing out troublemakers and cleaning up puke and piss. He mixed few drinks on football nights, but the taps flowed freely until closing time.

In the motion of bodies and faces Carroll noticed Heather Madison out of the corner of his eye. She was standing all alone among the heaving crowd, looking like a lost child. She was watching Carroll, unsure whether to approach.

Carroll smiled and waved her over to the end of the bar, away from most of the hubbub inside the restaurant proper.

As she sat down opposite him, Carroll leaned over the bar and kissed her full on the lips. The kiss lingered.

As their lips slowly broke apart, each felt a warm flush of satisfaction. It was good to be back together.

"You look great," Carroll couldn't help but notice. She sure knew how to fill out a pair of Levi's, every ripe curve accented by a pocket, a seam, a metal stud. She wore a simple black bodysuit underneath, which tastefully revealed the rest of her graceful lines.

She brightened. "Thanks."

"I'm glad you came hon, but I'm sorry it's our noisiest night," he shouted over a burst of cheers. "I was going to call you tomorrow when all this madness is over. Booker T. and the MGs are playing B.B. King's club this weekend and I've got a couple of good tickets. How about it?"

"You *are* well-connected, Carroll. Sure, I'd love to go."

A swell of voices rose in a cheer, as the crowd followed a field goal attempt.

"Ugh. I hate football," Heather said. "I hope that doesn't change your opinion of me."

"Quite the contrary, sweetheart."

"I figured a guy your size would love football."

"Nah, never cared for the sport. My old man, he was the one who loved football. Was always after me to play. I never could quite see the point. All that *hit, hit, hit* shit. Plus, I never met a coach I didn't think was some kind of goddamned idiot."

Carroll caught the sleeve of a waiter who had been helping out behind the bar. "Jay, my man. Can you take over for me for a little while?"

"Sure, no problem."

Carroll walked around the bar and sat on a stool next to her. He hugged her again and kissed her on the cheek. She was all sunbeams and smiles.

"Carroll, how did you get into arm wrestling?" Heather asked when conversation seemed called for.

"Well, I was born strong. *Real* strong. About ten times stronger than your average Joe Blow office worker. I guess I had to do something with it. God-given talent and all that shit. I saw an arm wrestling tournament on the news one night when I was a kid. I'm not bullshitting when I tell you I knew then and there I'd be up on that tournament stage some day."

"Was this before Steve Strong was famous?"

"It was when he was first getting known. Steve's my best friend in the sport, and I have no friends. I have lots of enemies, particularly one asshole named Scud Matthews, who managed to win the last Professional Arm Wrestling Association World Tournament. I happen to know Scud was heavy into the juice at the time, that's how he beat me."

"The juice?"

"Anabolic steroids. PAWA just last year got around to prohibiting steroid use. They felt it was too expensive to test everyone, and they don't make enough money to stand up to a lawsuit if they fuck up a report.

"Now they have a 10-panel drug test for every wrestler who places in a match. Each urine specimen goes through what they call a total chain of custody. If anyone tests positive for steroids it's re-verified through a more foolproof test that tells no lies. Mr. Scud was nothing but chum bait until he started juicing, then his arms blew up like hot air balloons. But now he's on his own, no robo arm to back him up. And I've got his fucking number."

"Didn't I read something in the paper about this guy, Scud?"

"He's always getting in trouble hustling in small towns. He nearly killed a guy over in Pine Bluff, Arkansas last month, but he beat the rap because even the locals admitted he more or less acted in self defense. What they don't know is that the real reason he was there was to psych me out."

"How could he psych you out all the way over in Pine Bluff?"

"Sweetheart, long-distance psyching is what this game is all about."

Chapter 5

"He doin' it again, Mr. Jacob."

"Who's doing what again?"

"That big white man wit' the big Popeye arms in the lobby again messin' wit' the chairs."

"Jeez. I thought we were rid of that guy. Get Bobby in Security."

❖   ❖   ❖

The lobby in question was that of The Peabody Hotel in Memphis, not inaccurately referred to in all hotel promotions as The South's Grand Hotel. The Peabody is renowned the world over for its trained mallard ducks that swim in the lobby fountain, as they have done every day for the last sixty years. The daily entrance of the ducks, which ride down the elevator from their luxury quarters on the Peabody roof to the lobby, and march single file to the fountain, never fails to attract a throng armed with a million watts of flashpower.

"The Mississippi Delta begins in the lobby of The Peabody Hotel," a quotation nearly always wrongly attributed to William

Faulkner, only partially explains the history and powerbrokering of the Peabody lobby and its focal points, the bar and its fountain. Like The Plaza in New York, every person of influence in the South sooner or later sips a drink in that lobby. Million-dollar handshakes go down over bourbon and branch water every day.

Honeymooning at the Peabody is *de rigueur*, and adultery isn't taken seriously in Memphis unless it is conducted under the watchful eyes of the lobby patrons. More babies were conceived on the monogrammed percale sheets of the Peabody Hotel during World War II than any other hotel in the world, because every American soldier with a bone injury was shipped to Memphis for treatment by the city's world-class orthopedic surgeons. The hookers who frequent the hotel are the classiest this side of Hollywood. So classy, in fact, that only seasoned bell captains can spot one.

If there was one place in Memphis, Tennessee to get attention, it was the Peabody lobby. Wearing a conservative grey suit with a silk paisley tie, a tailored Egyptian cotton oxford white shirt, and black Johnston & Murphy oxfords polished to a blinding glare, Carroll Thurston nodded as he walked past the Peabody doorman, entered the grand lobby, and carefully removed his suit jacket. He rolled up his shirt sleeves, loosened his tie, and placed two table chairs on either side of him.

"May I take your order, sir?" asked an attractive waitress with a hairstyle that reminded Carroll of cellophane Easter grass.

"Yes. It's 2:07 right now. In exactly thirty minutes bring me two Killian's and two glasses of water, no ice. Bring it exactly at 2:37 and you'll get a twenty dollar tip. One minute before or after and you get nothing. *Comprendè?*"

Her head jerked toward the clock. "Yes sir!"

Carroll seized one of the squat, amply-upholstered chairs in each arm and slowly swung each chair over his head to a semaphore's ten o'clock/two o'clock position, as if he were giving the Y sign for the song "Y.M.C.A."

Carroll's size had already captured the notice of every customer in the lobby. When he lifted the two chairs, however, he
created a genuine commotion. People argued that he must be
some lunatic off the streets downtown or an entertainer of
some sort, hired by the Peabody for their amusement.

A crowd gathered as Peabody personnel poured out of their
work stations.

Through it all, Carroll stood stock still. The look of catato-
nia on his face kept anyone from approaching, including the
security personnel who hovered like honeybees, buzzing into
their walkie-talkies.

Carroll's jaws were clinched in an evil grimace and his teeth
were bared like a Doberman dog's. Sheets of sweat began to roll
off his deeply furrowed brow. The veins in his neck stood out
taut as guy wires.

His shirt was soon soaked through. The chairs did not waver
a fraction of an inch.

The Peabody manager had instantly phoned the Memphis
Police Department, which dispatched their elite TACT Squad to
the hotel. Arriving in only minutes, the TACT Squad comman-
der was escorted to the trouble.

"Hell, don't you know who that is?" he asked Ira Jacob, the
Peabody manager.

"No. He's been here before and created a disturbance, but I
have no idea who he is."

"He's Carroll Thurston, the world champion arm wrestler who
lives in midtown. He must be in training for a tournament. Several
of the boys here know him. He's a bartender over at The Bombay
Bar. The way I look at it, Ira, he's putting on a free show for you.
Boys, have a seat in the lobby. Darlin', how about a round of
Cokes for all my boys. Put it on Ira's tab. Make mine a Diet and
puts lots of ice in it.

"How does Thurston do that?" he chuckled as he grabbed a
fistful of Goldfish crackers.

❖ ❖ ❖

The "how" was simple enough; it was pure hate. A hate that had no bottom to it. A hate focused entirely on Bernie Kelso, Carroll's old boss, and a local legend. Kelso was the sole owner of the Kelso Agency, the nation's fifth-largest advertising agency. Kelso was the son of Gerald Kelso, who had founded the agency after the Second World War and presided over its growth as it became a power in the Mid-South. Bernie, his only son, was far more driven and fanatical than the old man, and even dropped out of college because he couldn't stand not making money.

In the sixties the young Bernie usurped his father's authority by taking over hiring and firing decisions. By paying above-market salaries and searching continually for the best creative talent, the Kelso Agency acquired many of the most lucrative national accounts. Although high-priced even by New York standards, the Kelso Agency delivered excellence no matter what the assignment or deadline.

The fact that Bernie Kelso made virtual slaves of his employees while the turnover rate among his hand-picked talent exceeded two hundred percent a year had no impact on either him or his bottom line. Bernie seldom paid vacation time, sick leave, maternity leave, or long-term disability because no employee was around long enough. No one was ever fired. They all quit.

Everyone left, not because they couldn't stand the work load, which was murderous, but because they hated Bernie Kelso's fat little guts. His temper fits were the stuff of a madman's nightmares. Every employee had a horror story and every employee had a Maalox addiction. Even in their dreams they couldn't escape the wrath of Kelso.

Carroll Thurston had been one of the South's most honored ad copywriters. Because he had utter disdain for the cute and the clever, Carroll was a master of the telling anecdote and solid lead that connected with the reader. Although ad agencies were filled with so-called experts who firmly believed no one ever actually read an ad, Carroll knew that ads never boosted client sales unless the reader read the whole thing. Carroll's ads all read like superbly-crafted short stories with the kind of symmetry of prose only an experienced pro could provide. Carroll Thurston got results, and no one cared that the arty-farty art directors found his ads visually dull.

The Kelso Agency had tried many times to recruit him, but Carroll was warned away by all his contacts in the business. He figured he and Kelso would lock horns within minutes. Then they made him one of those *Godfather* offers.

Carroll figured that after two years at the agency he could pay off his mortgage and devote his life entirely to arm wrestling—a goal he desperately wanted to reach. Without a sizeable nest egg, Carroll could never hope to make it on the measly $10,000 to $20,000 dollars per year the number-one ranked wrestler could get from prize money and endorsements. That's why so many professionals, like Scud Matthews, hustled on the side. It was so rare to be recognized as a champion out in the boonies that a smart hustler could double or triple his earnings. Tax-free at that.

But Carroll had long ago given up on wrestling amateurs in bars. It just wasn't worth the effort and argument, and a lot of losers took losing very personally. Personally enough to shoot your ass.

So Carroll kept a civil tongue and put up with the Twilight Zone corporate weirdness of the Kelso Agency. When the boss screamed in his face for twenty minutes because his memo margins were off one silly fucking millimeter, he yessirred and nosirred his way past it, even though it ate his guts for days. But when he put in a seventy-hour work week to knock out a major ad campaign, only to get called down for missing a deadline on a worthless make-work monthly report, he drew his line in the sand.

Kelso called him into his office and immediately backed him against the wall. Although only five-foot-three, Kelso was a master of physical and psychological intimidation. He worked himself into a violent rage so effectively that his victims were reduced to mute spasms. Kelso spewed and sputtered and specks of spittle flew. Carroll took it all in stride until Kelso accused him of being a lazy failure and poked him in the chest with his forefinger. Carroll calmly walked over to the large, highly-polished mahogany conference table, and with his bare hands ripped out a three-foot section of the table top.

"Run that by me again, you little bald-headed bastard," he snarled as he tapped him in the chest with the wood section.

Kelso ran like a stripe-assed ape.

After that, bartending looked pretty good. It was okay money, a night owl's hours, and an endless supply of women. And there were no more Kelsos.

Even though every muscle in his hands, arms, and shoulders burned as if blasted by an acetylene torch, Carroll held steady by centering the yapping face of Bernie Kelso square in his mind. He mentally focused on Kelso's interminable motivational meetings such as the annual Magnificent Monday where Kelso gloated over his employees by handing out scrawny bonus checks. He visualized Kelso's explosions when someone dared to nod off during a meeting and how his phalanx of vice presidents applauded even his goofiest suggestions.

The memories fueled the hate. It was hate that kept the chairs aloft for thirty solid minutes. Even strong laboring men couldn't last beyond five minutes. Few weightlifters could make it beyond fifteen.

The carpet under Carroll was pocked with sweat. His joints ground together like metal on metal. Around 2:30 the chairs had begun to vibrate, at first with just mild tremors, then wild jumps and jolts, which elicited oohs and aahs from the crowd. A growl began in the back of Carroll's throat that grew into an ear-rending roar as the last minute ticked off.

The waitress cautiously approached with his order of beers and water.

"Excuse me sir, uh, sir? It is *exactly* 2:37."

With a final scream that stopped all business on the mezzanine and backed the waitress at least a yard, Carroll with great deliberation lowered the two chairs to tumultuous applause and whistles.

Carroll reached into his jacket pocket, took out a tiny lace handerkerchief and daintily dabbed his face. He took a Killian's, upended it and drained it off in one long swallow. He then let loose a belch loud enough to startle customers on the second floor.

"'Scuse me."

He chased it with a glass of water.

He held up thirty dollars rolled between his first two fingers. The waitress wasted not a second in snatching it.

Carroll slumped into one of the chairs and started on his second Killian's. Although the crowd couldn't tell, Carroll's arms were so weak with fatigue he could barely put the bottle to his mouth.

The stunt with the chairs was bound to get press, especially since the TACT Squad was called out. That was good. In addition to exciting a crowd, the chair stunt was a great training exercise. The biceps, the triceps, deltoids, shoulders—all muscles of great importance to a professional arm wrestler—were thoroughly stressed and conditioned. However, the real hidden benefit was the exceptional workout it gave the muscles in the wrist, hands, and fingers. Having hands and fingers of steel was critical to Carroll's own particular style of arm wrestling, which incorporated strategy, surprise, strength, and speed in equal measure. Carroll often gained the psychological advantage when opponents felt a grip like iron bands around theirs.

Finished with his drinks, Carroll stood again and was met with another wave of applause. He bowed and made a graceful sweeping gesture with his arm.

"Well, it's time for Oprah," he said as he picked up his jacket and left.

Chapter 6

Steve Strong was skin-popping his morning steroid cocktail when the doorbell rang.

With the syringe still sticking out of his arm, he thundered to the front door and yanked the door knob with all the muscle he could put behind it.

It was dead-bolted.

Letting loose with a string of curses, he grabbed the door knob with both hands and kicked against the door framing repeatedly with his feet until the deadbolt finally gave way with a loud crack from the wall.

"What the *fuck* do you want!?" Steve Strong screamed into the faces of the trespassers, who had foolishly ignored the warning sign posted on his front door.

Four Girl Scouts stared back at him in stark terror, their Girl Scout cookie boxes still held in the sales presentation manner they had been taught.

It took a second or two, but Steve realized he had made a terrible mistake. These were just little girls, for God's sake, Girl

Scouts trying to sell Girl Scout cookies. He loved Girl Scout cookies. It had been years since he had eaten any.

He began to cry.

"Girls, I didn't mean to scare you," he sobbed. "Okay? Do you forgive me?"

The girls looked at each other and without speaking all nodded yes.

"You're selling Girl Scout cookies, huh?" He wiped his eyes and nose on his t-shirt.

The Girl Scouts nodded again.

"What flavors do they come in?"

One girl cleared her throat and timidly recited the various offerings of Girl Scout cookies: Samoas, Thin Mints, Do-Si-Dos, Julietts, Trefoils, Chalet Cremes, Tagalongs.

"Sweetheart, I love Girl Scout cookies so much I want to buy a box of each. Okay?" He broke down again.

"Don't cry mister. We'll put you down for one of each. The orders will come in in six to eight weeks."

"That's fine, that's fine." He sniffed and reached out to pat their little heads. "I can't wait."

Steve closed the door as best he could and went to take a shit. He took a shit at least ten times a day and each time felt like knotted dock ropes were being dragged through his bowels. He hadn't shit a solid turd in six or seven years, since he began shotgunning steroids and anything else he could get his hands on that built muscle mass.

At first they worked like miracles. Steve Strawn had become Steve Strong as a result, featured on magazine covers, Wheaties boxes, commercials too numerous to remember, even clowning with Johnny Carson on *The Tonight Show*.

Now his knees felt like K-Y Jelly, his testicles had shrunk to the size of Milk Duds, and his piss came out the color of stagnant water.

He hadn't been seen at an arm wrestling tournament in over

two years. The rumor mill said he was dying of AIDS. At times he laughed to himself that at least they had the first part right.

Steve Strong had in fact looked death in the eye on more than one occasion and responded by bubbling up another hypodermic of steroids or whatever else would give him an edge—Anadrol, Dianabol, Bolasterone, Aldactazone, Ritalin, Triacana, Primobolan, Parabolin—all to prove to himself he was still Steve Strong. He wasn't so sure anymore.

Pain was a constant weight he carried. He took a portable pharmacy of painkillers everywhere he went. He had eaten so much high caloric bodybuilding food—cardboard-tasting candy bars and bogus mineral supplements—that his stomach was a roiling, heaving mess. He could only sleep an hour or so at a time, and the sleep deprivation coupled with the nagging pain and years of steroid abuse made him a dangerous man.

In Nashville, where Steve Strong lived and was loved like a major league sports hero, the local police had been alerted to his increasingly erratic behavior. When a waiter failed to bring his meal in a timely manner, Steve grabbed him by the collar and slapped him until he bawled like a baby. He totalled out his high-performance Jeep Cherokee by ramming it into the car of a driver who was stupid enough to flip him off on the expressway. Steve Strong's celebrity status kept him from doing any jail time, but the patience of the police was beginning to wear thin.

❖　❖　❖

Steve Strong had not only ruled the sport of arm wrestling for nearly twenty years, but, as Arnold Swartzenegger had done for competitive bodybuilding, he had put it on the map. Steve's movie-star good looks and charismatic personality captivated a documentary filmmaker, Marris Boyles, who catipulted him to fame in the cult classic, *Wrist Action*. Steve had proven himself a master of self-publicity, ingratiating himself with the Studio 54 crowd in New York. Andy Warhol did a famous portrait of Steve Strong's arm titled *The Man With the*

Golden Arm that was on permanent display at The Museum of Modern Art.

Steve also had no qualms about letting select fashion brokers wrestle something besides his arm. They, in gratitude, groomed him for stardom and introduced him to the world of ultra-desirable women. His long-enduring romance with a gap-toothed supermodel was fodder for the tabloids for years.

But Steve always put the sport first.

The writers for *Sports Illustrated,* who were long accustomed to the arduous training regimens of boxers, were nonetheless impressed with the severity of Steve Strong's workouts. He exercised at least six hours a day, beginning with a five mile run and ending with pulls with a robotic arm designed for him by engineering students at M.I.T. Steve exercised not only his arm and shoulder muscles, but spent hours exercising the fingers and thumb of his right hand. Consequently, his whole right arm was about one-third larger than his left.

He also worked exhaustively to perfect his timing and reflexes, changing the game from occasional prolonged standoffs over the wrestling table to warp-speed takedowns. Steve was also responsible for adding strategy to the game, developing explosive moves such as the widely-imitated over-the-top and drag-down styles. PAWA was essentially founded by Steve Strong, who tirelessly promoted and plugged the organization. Steve's goal was to make arm wrestling an Olympic event. At this alone, he had failed, although through his ceaseless efforts he had elevated the sport far beyond the 'tonks and roadhouses in which it was born and flourished.

Perhaps most importantly, Steve Strong had added much-needed showmanship to a sport that bored the masses. *Wide World of Sports* had turned down all invitations to cover major arm wrestling tournaments. When they aired a ten-minute segment taken from the *Wrist Action* documentary, calls poured in to the network's switchboards demanding more on arm wrestling and Steve Strong. Thus, a star was born who went from five hundred-dollar prize winnings to six-figure advertising endorsements and gag matches on TV with Johnny Carson.

Steve had moved to the top rank of arm wrestling with seeming ease for a man in his early twenties. Arm wrestling, unlike almost any other physically demanding sport, was not a young man's game. Strength gains in the necessary arm and wrist muscles were possible into a puller's late fifties. The average age of top champions was from 35 to 40 years old. Young men seldom had acquired the necessary strength or smarts to displace the older pros.

Unlike almost all other arm wrestlers, however, Steve Strong approached the sport on an intellectual as well as physical level. He consulted orthopedic doctors, biochemists, pharmacologists, psychologists, motion scientists, and motivational experts. From them he developed his split-second takedown approach and his psych-out tactics.

In the beginning, Steve Strong psyched out opponents by slapping and pounding the regulation Jeffrey wrestling table and making no pretense at sportsmanship. He worked himself into a fine rage before ever touching his arm to the table. This so unnerved most of his opposition that he breezed through the finals.

When those tricks lost their effectiveness, he devised new ones.

Sniffing smelling salts was good for several years, and then he came up with his masterstroke. As filmed in *Wrist Action* and subsequently seen throughout the world, Steve approached the wrestling table with a drop-dead gorgeous woman on each arm. One woman removed the crown he wore, the other removed a flowing cape. They then in turn slapped him beet-red in the face until he was mad enough to pry nails out of the wall with his bare teeth. The opposition went down like fifty-dollar whores.

In more recent years Steve would open a can of Quaker State motor oil and drain it down his throat in front of hundreds of sickened spectators. What no one knew was that Steve had made a secret deal with an artist friend who duplicated the oil can label and pasted it over cans of maple syrup. Steve also believed the sugar rush that resulted gave him yet another edge.

Those were the glory days, and they were long gone. A dozen doctors had warned Steve Strong that he had overloaded nearly every major organ in his body. His liver and pancreas stood a good chance of seizing up and shutting down if he kept fueling up with steroids and worse. Steve knew he had a king-size monkey on his back, a monkey that was biting deep.

In the last PAWA World Championship, he had washed out so early that it caught everyone by surprise. He had looked good, but felt like shit and performed like some meatbag beginner. Only Carroll Thurston, the single arm wrestler he had ever taken under his wing, knew what was wrong. Carroll had told him point-blank that he was nothing but a junkie, and he was right.

Now Steve Strong was one sad sack sonofabitch, wracked in pain like a little old man, barely able to wipe himself as he sat straining his bowels on the toilet. As he stretched to reach the crack in his ass with another Tucks pad, he felt a jolt and a shot to his kidneys that knocked him to the floor. Gasping for breath, Steve felt blows like steel-toed boots connecting deep inside his abdominal cavity. He could neither speak nor move, only react.

Hours later the 911 operator received a call from the fashionable Brentwood suburb of Nashville. All she could hear was a whisper repeated over and over. "Momma, help...momma, help...momma, help." The paramedics found the great Steve

Strong lying face down on the bathroom floor in a state of near paralysis, a pool of diarrhea around his mid-section. A succession of increasingly expensive specialists monitored his vital signs. He remained in the intensive care unit for six days.

Consciousness came and went like a television coming into focus then abruptly shut off. Somehow Steve Strong had figured out that he was in a hospital with tubes running in and out of every hole in his body—not to mention a few new ones. Sometimes he was in unspeakable pain and other times he felt as if he were being slowly covered in a blanket of warm milk. There were electronic sounds of high-tech equipment all around him, oxygen bubbling peacefully in the background, and an admixture of voices, none of which he quite recognized.

One afternoon he came to the groggy realization that he had been awake for quite some time. Although not all at once, everything in the room began to take on a familiar feel, as if he had been there for ages. He focused his eyes on someone sitting in a chair next to his bed, someone he was sure he knew.

"Steve, I wish you could see yourself. Damn if you couldn't scare a buzzard off a gutwagon."

"Carroll, is that you, boy?"

"Present and accounted for, *sahib*. I was on my way to the Tennessee Special Olympics here in Nashville when I got word about you. You know, you were about a frog-hair from checking out. Those steroids and other shit you've been dumping into you have just about done your ugly ass in. There's no way you can ever touch that stuff again."

"What do the docs say is wrong with me?"

"The question is, what's *not* wrong with you. Let's see, your kidneys are full of stones, you've got damage to the pancreas and liver. Your heartbeat is irregular and you've got the colon from hell. They've had you in a gizmo called a lithotripter trying to break up the kidneystones. Your colon, they tell me, was packed like paté with white chalky-looking shit.

"Steve, if you're going to make it, you've got to be a good boy from now on. No more steroids, no uppers, or any of that power-food crap you eat."

Steve forced a small grin. "Know where I can join an AA group?"

"Man, you *are* an AA group."

"I was just into a little self-improvement is all."

"Yeah, I heard about the waiter you self-improved."

"Hey, at those prices I demand service."

"Tell that to the waiters at the Brushy Mountain Penitentiary."

Steve weakly motioned for Carroll to come closer. Carroll walked over and leaned down.

Steve whispered. "I ain't down for the count yet, coach. Watch me. I'll make it back to the top. This will all be just another bad memory. Steroids get to be a nasty habit, but you wouldn't know. PAWA tests now anyway. But old habits die hard. Speaking of which, you still need a gimmick. Besides me, you're the best there is. But old Scud is a lot more fun to watch. You need an attention getter."

"Well, I've got a good one now. Can you keep a secret?"

"Sure."

Carroll leaned close to his ear and whispered, "Cockroaches."

They looked at each other and both began to grin. Steve Strong began a phlegmy chuckle that he had to cut short. It hurt too much to laugh.

❖ ❖ ❖

Over the next several weeks Steve Strong began to show signs of recovery. He pissed over a dozen B.B.-sized kidneystones. And he shit a single solid turd, about the size of a Tootsie Roll bite.

Chapter 7

Carroll was lying on a psychiatrist's couch in a totally dark-ened room. Suddenly, he was bathed in bright light as was the psychiatrist who, it dawned on him, was Frasier Crane, the lovable neurotic from the television sitcom.

This Frasier Crane was anything but lovable. He wore a malicious smirk on his face.

"Of course, Mr. Thurston, your diagnosis is simplicity itself. Any first year psychology student could have ascertained that you suffer from *cantrathriptaterraphobia*, an unreasoned fear of becoming a cripple, a 'special' person, as it were."

"What can you do for me Doctor Crane?"

Frasier stood up and laughed heartily. He had a long carving knife in each hand that he whetted together.

"Elementary my dear man. All we have to do is...turn *you* into a cripple." He snapped his fingers. "Boys!"

A dozen assistants in white lab coats seized Carroll and began drilling and hammering at every major bone. His screams came out muted. No one could hear them. In seconds he was covered head to toe in heavy clamps and braces, with bloody bone pins sticking out like a pincushion. Pain lashed every fiber of his body.

He was then propped up by the assistants and forced to walk down a dark hall. Each step was an unbearable torment and the sound, a massive, horrendous clanking, got louder and louder. He looked down the hall. The boy was there, clanking towards him, arms outstretched, with an angel's smile.

The clanking got louder and louder as Carroll woke up screaming, the roar still in the ears of his mind.

Chapter 8

The first sounds Carroll Thurston heard as he walked from the parking lot to the entrance of Vanderbilt Stadium in Nashville for the Tennessee Special Olympics were the heated voices of two women. The ladies had attracted considerable attention and mediators were trying, to no avail, to calm them down.

"Sorry, but I just can't agree. I think it's total *bullshit* to call our children *special* in these fund-raisers. It's like we're trying to pretend that everything's just fine. And it isn't just fine."

"So you're telling me these children aren't special?" the other lady replied.

"That's my point. Every child is *special*, whether the child has a handicap or not. Why hide from the truth?"

The other woman shook her head no. "We don't want our children stigmatized, that's why. Jerry's Kids face enough as it is without being called 'retarded' or 'crippled'."

"Jerry's Kids? Oh please!"

"Ladies, ladies," a man wearing a referee's uniform interrupted. "Can't we discuss this some other time? We're here to all have a good time today and let our kids show off a little bit. C'mon, how about it?"

Both women turned and angrily walked away.

Christamighty, thought Carroll. Is this going to be a shitty day or what?

Carroll suddenly felt two arms reach around his waist and he jumped back, startled. The person reached around him again and hugged tight, then looked into Carroll's eyes and said, "I wuv you."

It was a boy of about fifteen or sixteen. With his thick neck and midsection Carroll could plainly see it was a Down's syndrome child. The boy would not let go. Dumbfounded, Carroll stood there red-faced, not knowing what to do. God, why hadn't he backed out of this Special Olympics crap when he had had the chance?

Finally, Carroll awkwardly put his arms around the boy and began to hug him back. He cleared his throat and looked around to see if anybody was watching.

"I love you too, partner. What's your name?"

"Bywon."

"Byron? That's a nice name. Are you going to arm wrestle me today?"

"Okay."

Byron smiled and put his hand into Carroll's. He stood there blissfully content to hold hands and watch the passing parade.

"I see you've met my son?"

It was Pamela, according to the name tag she wore, the woman who had objected to her child being classified as special.

"I apologize if you've been bothered," she said. "I stepped away for a few minutes..."

"Think nothing of it, ma'am. Byron and I have become good buddies already. I asked him if he wants to arm wrestle with me today?"

"Oh, you're the man from the arm wrestling association?"

"Yes ma'am. The name's Carroll Thurston. I'm the second ranked pro on the PAWA circuit. I've been tapped by the association to work with the kids today."

She held out a slender hand. "I'm Pamela McTeague. Pleased to meet you. Shall we take you to the arm wrestling station?"

"I'd be honored."

Still holding Carroll's hand, Byron lunged forward. "I know da way."

"Slow down just a bit hon," Pamela sweetly scolded. "This is Mr. Thurston's first visit to our Olympics. We don't want to wear him out too early."

"How did you know it was my first time here?" Carroll asked her as they walked across the crowded football field.

"Oh, I've seen the look many times," she smiled good-humoredly. "Kind of like jackrabbits frozen by headlights. You're not used to being around handicapped children are you?"

"No, not really. Or *special* ones either." He glanced at Pamela to gauge her reaction, to see if she could take a mild ribbing.

"Oh, you heard me get on my soapbox today?" she laughed and colored slightly, a good sign as far as Carroll was concerned. "Well, well, you've seen my charming side, then."

"That took some real guts, all kidding aside," Carroll told her.

"Thanks," she blushed again. "Here's your booth Mr. Thurston. This is Janice Edwards, she'll be your guide today." Janice and Carroll greeted one another and shook hands.

"We've got track and field events to attend now, Mr. Thurston," Pamela said. "If you like, I'll bring Byron by later before we leave." She gave Carroll a look.

"By all means," Carroll answered, quickly responding to her cue. "And please, call me Carroll."

"Alright then," she smiled. "Byron, tell Carroll bye for now."

"Bye fowuh now."

"See you later, cowboy."

Carroll kept his eyes fastened on the mother's backside,

admiring the slow, rolling sway of her hips, as she walked away with her son. He caught himself and for a moment began to feel guilty. He had a pretty good thing going with Heather Madison and now here he was striking up an acquaintance, an innocent acquaintance, surely, with this lady, Pamela McTeague. Heather had surprised him. She defied the stereotype of the self-obsessed salon beauty. She was smart as a whip, witty in a town in which wit had no currency, cultured, the most sensitive human being he had ever known. The downside to her personality was that she latched on fast and tight. He had no room to operate within her sphere of influence, which seemed to include the whole city of Memphis. Although Carroll was known to practically all of the advertising community in the city and to the small sub-culture that knew him as a professional arm wrestler, he was relatively anonymous to the public at large. Despite a few articles in *The Commercial Appeal*, the hometown newspaper, he was seldom recognized by strangers around town.

Not so with Heather. She may as well have been a local celebrity since she could go to no restaurant, movie, or nightclub without a dozen people making a fuss over her. Hairdressers, especially those who worked the more exclusive salons, were regarded as modern day Aphrodites, bestowing beauty to those deemed worthy. Carroll did not enjoy the attention.

Carroll found it difficult to reject either Heather's affections or the possibility of Pamela's, for however short a period of time. He found the thing called love too rare a commodity to be dismissed simply because he was in a loving relationship with someone else. This had caused him untold grief in his life and ended his only marriage, a brief matrimony during his senior year at the University of Memphis that didn't make it to the six-month mark. Although married, he just couldn't end a relationship with a journalism coed that had mushroomed into a full-blown affair. The problem was he truly loved both women, was crazy about them in fact, and there was no way around it. Of course, no one else saw it quite that way. Particularly the divorce judge. Carroll couldn't find the logic of confining his love indefinitely to one woman, especially if there was someone else to share it with.

It wasn't just a sex thing either. As far as Carroll was concerned, sex had become too faceless to give him the ego gratification he required. The parade of one-night stands satisfied his sexual appetites, it was true. But he wanted more out of a relationship than being a human dildo. Every long-term relationship he had was eventually sacrificed to a lover's insistence on monogamy. Heather was wound too tightly to ever let him off her leash. She would not understand.

By the afternoon, a succession of children had had a ball arm wrestling each other and Carroll. Carroll won over the children, and parents as well, by good-naturedly losing, often to comic effect. Some of the children could not get enough of him and stood in line over and over to beat the great arm wrestling champ. Carroll proved to be an excellent actor.

A hugely-muscled man in a sleek modified wheelchair rolled up to the wrestling table and held up his hand to begin.

"Let's have at it, you son of a bitch."

There was a glimmer of recognition.

"Barry Daniels? Is that you?" Carroll asked, incredulous.

"Sure as shit, son. I take it the number-one arm wrestler had better things to do today?"

"Yeah, like getting his prostate gouged by his partner. God, how long has it been? At least fifteen years?"

Barry Daniels was, without question, one of the greater athletes Carroll Thurston had known, although few would have considered him an athlete at all. Carroll would never forget the sensation Barry created his first day of their sophomore year at Sheffield High School. Several chair-bound students had been transferred to Sheffield since the school was brand new and had all the latest ramps, hardware, and conveniences to accommodate wheelchairs. Until Barry's arrival, most of the handicapped students had seemed sickly and frail. Barry, however, impressed everyone from day one during Phys-Ed by nonchalantly popping a wheelie and holding it for a solid hour. No one, the coach included, could keep his eyes off that wheelchair. Barry was the talk of the school for days. He insisted on taking P.E. with the other boys and could kick anyone's ass in free-throws, volleyball serves, or bomber forward passes.

One of his wheelchair stunts literally caused several girls to faint. During study hall one afternoon, when the teacher stepped out of the school auditorium (where study hall was held), Barry popped a wheelie and began rolling down the center aisle. He had started at the top of the auditorium, which sloped at a twenty-degree decline, and began to pick up considerable speed. By the time he had rolled to the bottom, he was flying, a crash imminent. At the last possible second, he grabbed the arm of a chair on the front row, whipped around at a ninety degree angle, and neatly averted plastering himself against the stage. The screams and gasps were so loud that teachers came running from every direction. In the ensuing pandemonium, three girls were administered smelling salts, and Barry Daniels was given a three-day board suspension. He was a hero.

He was also a handgun victim.

Although his father had told him a hundred times to never touch the gun in the top drawer, something that shiny and awful proved too great a temptation. The way Barry remembered it, although he knew in his heart it could not be so, he merely picked it up and held it in his small hands. For no reason, no reason at all, there was a flash of fire followed by the loudest noise he had ever heard. Then there was a terrible warmth. Terrible because the warmth was so inviting.

Choosing between life and that final comforting warmth was not an easy decision for an eleven-year-old to make. There was so much shouting, from his parents, his doctors, his nurses, everyone who wanted him to live. He thought it would be so much easier to just slide away.

But he did live, even if he would never walk, never run, never know the pleasure of being inside a woman.

You could either love the chair or hate it. Barry decided he would learn to love it the minute the nurses put him in one. When the boys in the neighborhood popped wheelies on their Stingray bikes, Barry learned to do the same in his chair. He fell on his ass about a thousand times until he got it, but his friends assured him it was no easy matter mastering a wheelie on a bicycle either.

When the boys ran down the streets, Barry wanted to run alongside them. As a result, he developed tremendous arms and upper-body strength for a boy. If anything, he could soon go faster than his friends. He could also out-arm wrestle every boy in his age group. Until he met Carroll Thurston in high school and Carroll put him down in five seconds flat.

The two developed a mutual admiration even though Barry always suspected Carroll was uncomfortable with his handicap, a suspicion Carroll never admitted. They had hung out a few times during their senior year after Barry bought a souped-up Plymouth Roadrunner from a chairbound Vietnam vet. The Roadrunner would definitely haul ass big-time, and it was a magnet for other muscle cars and impromptu drag races. His Roadrunner was the scourge of Parkway Village, and he had the reckless driving citations to prove it.

Carroll had last bumped into Barry at the University of Memphis when he was a journalism student and Barry was taking courses in business. He had no idea what Barry'd been up to since.

"Man, what kind of rig have you got there?" Carroll asked. "That thing looks faster than that old Roadrunner you used to scare everybody with."

Barry laughed. "Whew, we had some times in that 'Runner,

didn't we? I'm surprised the cops didn't put out a hit on that car. Hell, I bet I could have bought a Rolls-Royce with all the tickets and fines they wrote me. It always fucked-up their heads when they had to lock me up, though. The guys in the tank, especially the drunks, didn't know what to make of a guy in a wheelchair either."

"Especially a guy in a wheelchair who wouldn't take any shit," Carroll reflected. "Remember that big spade you grabbed by the nuts when he tried to take your sandwich? That's one dude who won't be starring in porno movies any time soon."

Barry shook his head and laughed. "Yeah, I'll never forget the expression on his face when I gave him a little twist. You like the new chair, huh? It's a competition chair that I designed myself with the help of some engineering students at Christian Brothers University. It's made of a titanium alloy that's light as a feather. The axle bearings float in a type of liquid Teflon. It helped me set a world record."

"A world record? In what?" Carroll asked.

"In the wheelchair hundred-meter dash. I started competing about ten years ago, and I've won the American Nationals the last four years in a row. I've beat my own world record twice."

"God, that's great," Carroll said. "I always knew you were world class. Is there enough money in it to keep you going full time?"

"Nah. There's practically no money in it at all, no winnings or anything. Hustling sponsors, as I'm sure you know, is like a full-time job in itself. I get maybe a few grand a year at most. I still get a disability pension, but I work at Phil's Men's Shop as a sales clerk. I sell suits and slacks and so on, mostly to other wheelchair guys. The average tailor doesn't know shit about suiting up someone with a handicap. I've made it my job to come up with better ways to fit the hard-to-fit. I have an extensive client list now and I've been making a good living, no complaints."

"I used to be an advertising copywriter, but it drove me nuts," Carroll responded. "It paid well, but it took away from the arm wrestling. Now, I'm a bartender at The Bombay and life is a whole lot less complicated. I don't make even close to the money I did, but I aim to take the title next year at the PAWA Tournament and I need my days for training. What kind of training do you do?"

"I do five miles every morning and heavy weight training three days a week. You know where the old Charjean neighborhood is?"

"Sure, I went to grammar school in Bethel Grove right next to it."

"Then you probably know where Dwight Road is. It's got a great hill that's almost exactly one hundred meters from top to bottom. I bust ass going up it, then coast down and start over. About three good runs and I'm wasted. But it's great conditioning. Before a meet, I practice out at Halle Stadium on a flat track. I read about your training over at the Peabody."

"That was just a psych-out stunt. Psyching is an art in this sport. Anything that can throw off the opponent's concentration can win for you."

"When we get back to Memphis, we need to do some serious talk about training together."

"Okay. Let's do it."

❖ ❖ ❖

Carroll felt arms around his waist again. "Byron," Carroll responded without missing a beat. "How'd it go, my man?"

"Fine," he smiled and held up several ribbons.

"He ran like a little deer," Pamela chimed in, beaming. "Hi, Barry. How have you been?"

"Couldn't be better, Pammy."

"You two know each other?" Carroll asked.

"For years," Barry replied. "I hate to break up the party, but I've got a date tonight. Carroll, here's my card. It's got my home number on it. I'm serious about getting together back in Memphis. Take care of these two for me." He winked at Carroll.

"You got it."

Barry sped off in his chair.

"I've known Barry for at least ten years," Pamela said, "and I have yet to see him without a woman or running off to meet one. He's the most popular man I've ever known."

"That surprises me," Carroll replied. "I mean given his condition and all."

"Well, he is quite good-looking, you know, and he has a spectacular personality. And he, ahem, has other talents that may not seem so apparent."

"Surely you don't mean...after all he..."

"Let's just say he makes up for any inadequacies," she flushed red. "Use your imagination, Carroll."

He gave her a sideways glance and smiled, "Oh, I am."

She permitted herself an embarrassed smile back.

"Eat hambuhguhs wid us," Byron interjected.

"Well, thanks Byron, but I..."

"C'mon, Carroll, join us," Pam added. "It's a ritual that every time we come into Nashville—we live in Franklin just a few miles away—that we eat at Elliston's and stay over at the Howard Johnson. We could just drive back home, but Byron loves the Howard Johnson. The little soaps and shampoos send him into orbit. We'll treat you to the best burger and shake in the world."

How could he say no? Although she was no great beauty, Carroll found Pamela McTeague oddly appealing. She had no particular outstanding feature, but it all added up to something more. For one thing, she knew how to carry herself, and that made her all the more handsome. She also knew how to dress with taste, a shortcoming of many of the women Carroll encountered at The Bombay Bar. But what Carroll could not get over were her eyes. All the hurt in the world was pooled in the blues of her eyes—deep blue seas of unutterable sadness.

❖ ❖ ❖

They had been right. Elliston's Soda Shop was not only like entering a time warp—the entire place seemed frozen in the 1940's, from the fountain spigots to the blue plate specials—but the hamburger and milk shake were good, damn good. Carroll was surprised at how much fun he was having with them. In spite of the odd stares at Byron and at his own huge arms, Carroll actually felt comfortable and at ease with them. Byron was such a sweet, funny kid that his resistance had melted away. Pamela was great company, as engaging a conversationalist as he had ever met. She was an artist, more specifically a potter, and her work apparently sold in the hundreds of dollars. She had seriously studied the work of the great George Ohr, the so-called "Mad Potter of Biloxi," who at the turn of the century produced a body of work that was astonishing in its vision. Although Carroll knew little about this area of the art world, he found her stories mesmerizing. Her tales of meeting celebrity art patrons were frequently hilarious. Carroll didn't want her to stop.

"Momma, I gotta go to da bafwoom."

"Number one or number two, honey?"

"Numbuh one."

"Let's show Carroll what a big boy you are and see if you can go all by yourself. Don't forget to zip."

"Okay."

As Byron made for the bathroom, Carroll looked Pam in the eye and asked, "At the risk of offending, where might Byron's father be these days?"

"About ten miles from here in Memorial Park Cemetery."

Carroll sat like a stone. "Dead, I presume?"

"Very."

"I didn't mean to be so nosy…"

"It's okay. I don't blame you, I'd be curious too." She sighed. "It's just that the way he went was so...*odd*. I met Ted at one of my art shows, you know, one of those wine and cheese affairs. He was a young attorney not long out of law school and had just been hired by Dalton, Dalton, and Hirsch, a firm in Nashville.

"We got married, bought our home in Franklin, and continued our careers. I became pregnant, and at the end of the first tri-mester my ob/gyn began to suspect something wasn't quite right with the baby. The tests showed we were going to have a Down's syndrome child. We discussed the options, all of them, but decided to go ahead and have the baby.

"Ted wasn't the same after Byron was born. He began to work longer hours and wouldn't touch me for weeks at a time. When Byron was about a year old, Ted went up on the roof to nail a hole shut where squirrels had gotten into our attic. He fell off the roof and broke his neck. An accident, the police and the coroner said. A damned unlucky slip.

"The life insurance company did an investigation. An accident, they said. See, I didn't know it when he died, but he had taken out a half-million dollar policy. A panel from the insurance company grilled me about everything—our marriage, the baby, our sex life, you name it. I told them everything I could. The verdict was still that it was an accident. And I was left one very well-off widow. A well-off widow with a lot fewer friends, no family, and a Down's syndrome child to raise by myself."

As Carroll escorted Pamela and Byron to their car, Byron blurted out, "Spend da night wid us Carroll. Okay, *okay?*"

Carroll blanched and started to stammer something to save them all from embarrassment, but before he could utter a sound Pamela grabbed his wrist and looked into his eyes.

"Yes, come stay with us Carroll."

She couldn't be more serious.

"All right then."

"Oh boy-ee," Byron exulted.

At the Howard Johnson, Byron immediately flipped on the TV and flopped on one of the beds.

"Momma, put on Mowuk."

"Give me just a minute, sweetheart. He loves Robin Williams, calls him Mork. So I always bring a portable VCR and plug it into the back of the TV. He would watch the movies endlessly if I let him. Now I let him watch them only on special occasions as a reward. He did well today, so I'll let him watch one. How about *Garp* honey?"

"Okay."

"Byron also loves to watch Geraldo Rivera. He thinks he is the funniest man alive. He cackles whenever he talks, especially when Geraldo gets serious. Go figure. His favorite video is the one where Geraldo gets clobbered by the skinheads. I only play that one on *very* special occasions."

"I thought that one was pretty funny myself," Carroll said.

Later that night, Byron fell asleep in his pajamas watching *The World According To Garp*. Pamela and Carroll had watched too, sitting next to each other on the other bed. Finding Byron asleep, Pamela reached out and put a hand on Carroll's leg.

He answered by putting his hand around her soft, upturned neck and bent down to kiss her throat. She met his lips and they kissed long and deep. Carroll's head was swimming.

"Byron won't wake up. We can do what we want," Pamela whispered in his ear.

"I don't know, Pamela. I mean, what if he does wake up?"

"There's always the shower."

"With Byron here in the next room? I don't know. It would just be kind of *weird*. Not that there's anything wrong with weird, but..."

"Oh, all right, scaredy-cat. I guess you'll just have to watch television with me."

Long after Pamela had drifted off to sleep, Carroll lay wide awake next to her, feeling the warmth of her body, still smelling the tart sweetness of her perfume. It was a kind of hell lying there, wanting to touch, but not wanting to touch. Yet there was a satisfaction deep in his gut that he couldn't quite explain. Damned if he could figure it all out.

Chapter 9

Some days it just didn't pay to be in the porno business. Scud Matthews managed the Diddy-Wah-Diddy Adult Emporium & Video Arcade just off Bourbon Street in New Orleans' French Quarter. Just that morning he had received a shipment from Doc Benson's, the nation's largest distributor of adult novelty items. The box contained fifty gerbilling tubes, and Scud had spent the better part of the morning explaining to tourists the finer points of gerbilling. It was funny, he thought. When he explained it to them, they behaved as if they had been seized by some violent diarrhea. But they bought the damn tubes anyway.

Now he was having to disinfect the video booths for the third time that day. Old men were the worst. They would suck, fuck, or jerk anything. If they couldn't find a young woman or an old whore, they would settle for each other. Scud tried to keep only one person to a booth, but that was about as effective as a one-drink limit at Pat O'Brien's. Two people meant an automatic clean-up. A person alone might be tempted to whack-off, but was usually too fearful of being found out. If a customer had someone to grope with, however, orgasms would be had.

Married couples usually left little mess. They came prepared. Men together left drippings and smears everywhere. The lesbian booths were the best. Other than the occasional pubic hair, they were neat as shaved asses.

❖ ❖ ❖

While going through the morning mail, Scud noticed a linen paper invitation addressed to himself, Blanchard Riesling Matthews, in care of the Diddy-Wah-Diddy Adult Emporium & Video Arcade. The invitation read:

Your Presence and Participation Is Requested

In Honor of Anthony Norcross Bellini

To A Winner-Takes-All Arm Wrestling Exhibition

Five Thousand Dollar Prize Winnings

Tuesday, August 31, Midnight

Circle Q Truck Travel Plaza and Fuel Stop

West Memphis, Arkansas

R.S.V.P. (901) 555-8878

Scud immediately got on the phone to his manager, Itch, who ran Crutherd's Billiard Salon and Gumbo Parlor across Canal on Magazine.

"Itch, you ever heard of an Anthony Norcross Bellini?"

"Tony Bellini? Yeah, he runs the tittie bar scene in Memphis. Big into prostitution and drugs too. Whacks anybody who tries to muscle in. The feds have tried to shut him down for years, but can't get any charge to stick. He's an independent, but he's tight with the Candalino family here. Why you wanta know?"

"I just got an engraved invitation to a winner-take-all match in West Memphis. Says it's 'in honor of Anthony Norcross Bellini.' Says it'll pay five thousand bucks."

"Bellini will definitely be the ringmaster," said Itch. "He probably heard about the hustle in Pine Bluff and found a ringer somewhere."

"Think it's Carroll Thurston?"

"Not a chance," answered Itch. "Thurston doesn't like hustling, never has. He won't even do sideroom matches anymore. I think he wants to be the next Steve Strong."

"Yeah, well, who doesn't?"

"This could be tricky," Itch went on. "Bellini expects to win, unless he's floating side bets. If he expects to win, he won't take losing sitting down. He and his boys will be armed to the teeth, you can bet on it. But he's the sort of guy who likes to play big shot. If you win, he'll pay up in front of everyone. The bad part is he may try to get it back. It's good that he's an independent. He's on his own outside Memphis. The Candalinos wouldn't risk another RICO probe over any two-bit gig of Bellini's."

"I don't know Itch. Five thousand crispers sound pretty good to me right now. Could use it for training for the PAWA Tournament."

"We better be careful, that's all," Itch said. "Bellini is crazy, and he's mean. He likes to whip people with a big oak paddle with holes in it. Any of his people get out of line and he whips their bare asses raw. He's crippled up a few of his girls whipping them so hard. He's a different level of asshole than we're used to."

Chapter 10

The Circle Q Truck Travel Plaza and Fuel Stop in West Memphis, Arkansas more resembled an Air Force base than the typical greasy spoon road shack. The huge eighteen-wheeler rigs that filled the acres of concrete parking dwarfed all other vehicles that dared to enter the turf. Over thirty diesel pumps were in continual twenty-four hour use, pumping over a million gallons of fuel per week. Tanker trucks constantly off-loaded new cargoes of diesel. It was hard to keep up with the steady demand.

The Circle Q was one of several "super stops" located across the Mississippi River from Memphis in West Memphis. Like East St. Louis or Bossier City, Louisiana, West Memphis was a poor cousin to its bigger neighbor. Two major interstates, I-40 and I-55, intersected in West Memphis, and it was a natural stopover location. Restaurants advertising country ham and hot biscuits, waffle houses, a dog track, all catered to the industry that had become the bedrock of the West Memphis economy.

The super stops offered everything from barber shops and camouflage-colored condoms to fax machines and ATMs. At the Circle Q, a hot shower in a clean stall could be bought for five bucks and a trucker could watch an HBO movie free of charge on a big screen TV in the lounge. On the lot at night, whores crawled between the rigs, offering companionship at highly negotiable rates. The whores were the only major problem at the Circle Q. Dissatisfied customers frequently expressed their displeasure by beating the living shit out of the girls. Truckers sleeping off long, amphetamine-tanked runs didn't take kindly to whores banging on their windows for business either. More than one lot lizard, as the girls were commonly called, had been shot, although not seriously, and the authorities in West Memphis quickly swept such matters under the jurisdictional rug.

Big Ben Jessup worked out silently in a corner of the Circle Q lounge, table-curling two hundred-fifty pounds with his good arm. He was a household name in the central Mississippi area around Tupelo and New Albany. Big Ben cut and hauled firewood for a living and trimmed trees as a sideline. Crowds often watched as the bald-headed black man climbed tall, dead trees and cut them down section by section, usually holding a heavy chain saw in his one good arm. His left arm wasn't completely useless, it was just unnaturally small—about the size of a six year-old boy's—and powerless.

Aside from the bum arm, Ben Jessup was sculpted in muscles, and his good right arm was almost obscenely big. His feats of strength, such as snapping the jaws on pairs of handcuffs by flexing his wrist, were a staple of the community lore.

One of Tony Bellini's lieutenants was from the Tupelo area and had seen Big Ben Jessup outpull a mule at a county fair. Tony Bellini subsequently hired Big Ben for a series of strongman contests in his topless clubs. When he found out how good an arm wrestler he was, Bellini immediately dreamed of a match between Jessup and the hustler who won over in Pine Bluff, Scud

Matthews. A former PAWA contender, Bobby Simmons, whose career was cut short by a spiral fracture of the humerus that put him on the floor during a match, was recruited to coach Big Ben. Bobby Simmons had arm wrestled the best—Steve Strong, Scud Matthews, Carroll Thurston—but in terms of sheer arm power he had seen nothing like Ben Jessup's right arm. Although at 254 pounds, Ben wouldn't qualify as a super heavyweight under PAWA weight classifications, Simmons believed Jessup could outpower anyone.

The problem with Big Ben Jessup was that he simply didn't understand the game. He only knew flat out, and Simmons feared that a wily strategist like Scud Matthews could easily outmaneuver and outthink his dull-witted opponent. Arm wrestling wasn't just a show of strength, it was a show of how one *used* that strength. Jessup was like a batter who could hit everything but a curveball. If the game were kept simple, Big Ben Jessup could whip the world. But nothing was simple.

Bobby Simmons had warned Tony Bellini that it would be a mistake to stake too much on an unproven quantity like Ben Jessup. Bellini, however, considered Jessup his discovery and wouldn't hear a word that contradicted his high opinion of his man. Bellini had taken great delight in Jessup's training and workouts. He loved showing him off to high-roller customers.

Tony Bellini was a happy man. There were at least three hundred spectators in the Circle Q parking lot, each of whom had paid fifty dollars for the privilege of watching and betting at the unsanctioned arm wrestling match. It wasn't every day Tony's friends got the chance to see the world's number one arm wrestler go up against a ringer the likes of Big Ben Jessup. Tony had at least ten grand wagered on his man, and he had tipped his closest pals to bet big as well. When Big Ben won, Tony planned on rewarding him; he would pay him five hundred dollars. Ben Jessup knew nothing of the promised five thousand in prize winnings.

The arena on the parking lot had been created by boxing in the area with eighteen-wheelers. The entrance was through the only empty parking space. Bellini knew Scud Matthews could not resist the smell of five thousand dollars. Even when Scud demanded a PAWA referee and strict adherence to PAWA rules, Bellini knew he had him. Scud Matthews would return to New Orleans with empty pockets and his tail between his legs. Big Ben Jessup would then be able to pull in some real money as his ringer.

At five minutes 'til midnight, Bellini rang a bell to signal that the match would soon begin. A regulation Jeffrey table stood in the middle of the makeshift arena with the spectators crowding around for a good view. Big Ben Jessup was wearing a boxer's robe with Bellini's Alley Cat Club logo on it. Just seconds after the first call, Scud Matthews and Itch screeched to a stop at the entrance in an old, battered Chevy Nova that was spewing smoke out the exhaust. "Achy Breaky Heart" was blaring from the sound system.

Scud got out of the passenger side and did the "Achy Breaky" dance steps. He was wearing leather chaps with nothing on underneath except a jock strap. His bare butt was there for all the world and Arkansas mosquitoes. He wore a black T-shirt with the word TOP printed on it. Itch wore a matching T-shirt with the word BOTTOM.

Before they had taken two steps, two burly guards stopped them and one said, "Sorry, weapons check."

"Weapons check?" Scud echoed, outraged. "You assholes are packing. What if we don't like *your* fucking weapons?"

"Then tough shit," the guard with the cold, hooded eyes responded. "And this skinny little bastard has to pay fifty bucks to get in." He pointed to Itch.

"Tell Bellini he can take his five thousand and shove it up his ass," Scud said as he moved within an inch of the guard's face. "No manager, no match."

The guard stared him in the eye for an uncomfortable minute. He then slowly turned on his heels and walked over to Tony Bellini who was sharing a joke with a few cronies as they passed a hip flask of whiskey. The guard bent down and whispered in his ear and Bellini's expression abruptly soured.

Bellini stood up, put on a new smile big enough to reveal his gold back teeth, and walked towards Scud with open arms.

"Scud Matthews, my pleasure, my pleasure." He took Scud's hand, clasping with both of his own. "Tony Bellini, at your service. Sorry about the little inconvenience, gentlemen. Didn't realize you'd be bringing a friend. Say, you're the manager, huh?" He eyed their T-shirts.

"Among other things," Itch responded with a chill to his voice.

"Well, come on in, boys," Bellini continued. "I'd say things are about ready."

"You won't be needing this, Mr. Manager," the guard said without emotion as he removed a .38 Special from the small of Itch's back.

"Sorry, boys," Bellini apologized. "We're confiscating all sidearms, for everyone's protection, you understand. In case tempers run a little high. Some of these boys are a might high strung."

Itch turned to face the guard. "You are beginning to piss me off."

"Sorry, buttercup," the guard replied with the same cold wind in his expression.

"Now, now, let's be neighborly," Bellini said. "We've got a match to put on. What say?"

They walked through the crowd to the wrestling table amid a din of whistles and cheers.

Tony Bellini rang the bell again. Speaking into a bullhorn, Bellini announced, "In the cowboy chaps, weighing two hundred ninety-seven pounds, the number one Professional Arm

Wrestling Association champion, from New Orleans, Louisiana, Blanchard 'Scud' Matthews, Matthews.

"In the purple robe, the challenger, weighing two hundred fifty-four pounds, from New Albany, Mississippi, Benjamin Franklin 'Big Ben' Jessup, Jessup.

"Tonight's unsanctioned, non-title match will be refereed by Larry Dalton of the Professional Arm Wrestling Association. In accordance with PAWA rules, the match will be double elimination. All rules conform to PAWA regulations. I wish best of luck to both men."

Dalton, the referee, huddled with both wrestlers. "Okay, men. Keep it clean, no funny business, keep the top knuckle showing, keep the elbow in the cup and on the table at all times. Any questions? Good. Let's do it."

Big Ben Jessup couldn't quite figure out what the man had just said. He just wanted to wrestle and get it over with. It was late and he was tired and ready to go to bed.

As Scud and Big Ben began to position themselves at the Jeffrey table with their left hands holding onto a padded grip, Scud grinned and said "What's a big, ugly nigger like you doin' 'rasslin white boys?"

The effect was immediate and nuclear. "What'choo call me, you white muthafucka?" There was instant hate in Ben's face. He had been down this road too many times.

"I called you a big, ugly, stupid, stinking, spear-chunking, chittlin'-eatin', know-nothin' nigger."

"You!" Ben howled as he lunged across the table only to be restrained by his coach, Bobby Simmons, and a few of Bellini's men.

"Calm down!" Bobby Simmons shouted in his face. "Can't you see he's just trying to fuck with your head? Ignore him and concentrate on winning."

"Hey, I'm sorry man," Scud said with great sincerity. "I didn't mean to call you a stinking nigger. I can't really smell you yet."

"Shut up, Scud," the referee ordered. "Let's get a grip."

The wrestlers found their grip and settled into it. Big Ben glared at Scud with eyes like burning lasers.

"No loading 'til I say 'go'," said the ref. "Ready?"

"Ready," Scud said with assurance.

"Ready," Big Ben said, blinking back tears of rage.

"Go!"

Big Ben was met with only momentary resistance and slammed Scud Matthews with whistling power into the table. Scud picked up his hand from the table and shook it in pain. "Whew, you really got me good that time, Tobe." He cackled long and loud and walked towards Itch.

"Be back here in five minutes gentlemen," the referee announced.

"Five minute break," Tony Bellini spoke into the bullhorn.

❖ ❖ ❖

"This guy is solid nitro, man," Scud remarked to Itch. "I doubt I can power him down. Did you notice he just went straight to the mat? No moves at all. I can't believe Bobby Simmons coached him that way."

"Maybe Bellini's boy is as dumb as he looks," Itch replied. "He sounds like he just walked out of a Mississippi cotton patch. You need to use your weight to your advantage. Cut him inside and squeeze at the thumb base. I bet he won't know how to counteract."

Bellini rang the bell again. "Time, boys," he called from the bullhorn.

Scud walked straight to the table. Bobby Simmons whispered frantically into Big Ben Jessup's ear, patted him on the back, and walked him back to the table.

"Okay, fellas, get in position."

Scud seemed to have trouble getting a satisfactory grip. Just when Dalton was prepared to say "ready," Scud would back off, removing his elbow from the pad, bringing the match to a standstill. After the third time, the crowd began to jeer. Big Ben, already fighting an anger that had clotted in his throat, became even more confused and irritated by Scud's delays.

Finally the referee warned Scud, "No more stalling tactics, Matthews. Let's get things underway *now*. You don't want to tempt me with a forfeit."

"No sir," Scud answered.

Scud slowly worked his way into Big Ben's palm and began to squeeze his four fingers into the tender joint between Ben's thumb and forefinger. It was an old arm wrestling ploy designed to loosen an opponent's grip. Inexperienced wrestlers who hadn't exercised and strengthened their hand muscles were nearly always caught off-guard by the pain and subsequent loosening of grip it caused.

Big Ben's eyes grew wide as he felt bear claws digging into the pressure point at his thumb base. He had no idea how to respond, although he vaguely remembered Coach Simmons talking about such a thing.

"Ready?" the ref asked as he placed his hand over those of the wrestlers.

"No!" Scud answered. "Oxygen!"

Itch ran to him carrying a small bottle of oxygen with a face mask attached. He stuck it over Scud's face and gave him a couple of quick blasts.

"Ready!" Scud said with confidence.

"Ready," Big Ben said, glowering.

"Go!" the referee commanded as he removed his hands.

In a move faster than most eyes could follow, Scud jerked Big Ben's arm towards his chest. Ben's grip was so loosened by Scud's fingers that he could do nothing but go along. Putting his shoulder completely into the move, Scud caught Ben's arm off-balance and hammered it into the table. The total elapsed time was 01.54 seconds.

Big Ben blinked, certain that he must be seeing things. His

mind wouldn't accept the fact that he'd been taken down so fast. His mind wouldn't accept that he had been taken down at all.

"Damn!" he said.

Tony Bellini and Bobby Simmons exchanged worried looks. "Five minute break," Referee Dalton called out. "The score is now tied one and one. Next match determines the winner."

"Get over here!" Bellini ordered Big Ben. Simmons and Bellini immediately huddled with him. There was a murmur in the crowd; the betting odds had changed considerably.

"He'll be so worried about your fingers loosening his grip that he won't have any defensive moves in his head," said Itch. "Hit him with an over-the-top takedown. That should do the trick."

"Am I getting to him with the bullshit?" Scud asked.

"Are you kidding? He was so mad I thought his head would blow up. Keep the bit going. Meet me at the car as soon as you get the money. Make it fast too."

The bell rang. "Time, boys," Bellini called.

Scud and Big Ben faced off across the table, Scud leering and Ben glaring.

"Okay, get in position," the ref said.

As they were finding their grip Scud said in a sing-songy voice, "Nigger, nigger, *nigger*."

Ben Jessup hissed between gritted teeth, "Fucking f-faggot."

"That's right," Scud cooed. "When I get through kicking your ass I'm going to suck your sweet nigger dick." He flicked his tongue obscenely.

Big Ben was speechless, but the ref wasn't. "Knock it off, Matthews. This is my last warning about your big mouth."

"Okay, ref, sorry," Scud chuckled. Scud jerked his arm away from the table and feigned a sneeze into his right hand. He then blew his nose into his hand and began to put it back into position on the table.

"Foul!" at least a dozen people, including Tony Bellini, cried out.

Referee Dalton threw Scud Matthews a hand towel and ordered him to wipe his hands. "Matthews, this is your last stunt tonight. You so much as look cross-eyed at me or your opponent and you're outta here. Am I perfectly clear?"

"As clear as a sunny day, ref."

"All right then. Let's do it."

Big Ben backed off. "I ain't touchin' this snot-blowin' muthafucka. He cain't set there and call me no nigger to my goddamn face."

"Listen, son," Dalton told him. "If you refuse to go on you forfeit the match and lose. It's that simple. Matthews's hands are clean and he's been told to shut the hell up. Now it's up to you whether you want to let Matthews's baiting cost you the match. Egging on an opponent is not against the rules. It's a part of the game. You just have to be man enough to stand up to it."

"I don't care. I ain't touchin' him. Ain't nobody callin' me no nigger," Ben said defiantly.

Tony Bellini pushed forward and caught Big Ben square in the mouth with his open hand. Even Scud was shocked.

"By God you *will* put your arm on that table and you *will* wrestle. Words won't harm you, boy, but I know what will."

"Mr. Bellini, you're out of line…" Referee Dalton interjected.

"You just mind your own business and stick with refereeing this thing. Let's get going. We're wasting time."

Dalton chewed his lips and finally said, "Let's finish it fellas. I think we all want to go home tonight."

Without fuss or words they grabbed the handpegs, placed their elbows in the cups and quickly found their grip. Big Ben seemed in shock.

"Ready boys?"

"Ready."

"Ready."

"Go!"

Scud shifted all his weight to the ball of his right foot as his

left leg came up off the pavement. His shoulder moved into a
position squarely in the middle of the table, blocking any offensive move. It all ended in one continuous motion as Big Ben was
jackhammered into the touch pad with a deafening bang.

"Match!" Referee Dalton called. "Winner is Scud
Matthews."

Some of the spectators clapped and cheered; a great many
more moaned and booed.

Scud held out his hand. "My money, Bellini."

"You know son, I don't believe I like your attitude," Bellini
said quietly. "I don't like the way you play your game and I
don't like the way you behave. I feel embarrassed to have invit-
ed you. I don't believe you earned the prize winnings I put up.
You have insulted me, my wrestler, my family, my neighbors,
my friends. You have disrupted a fine sporting event and the
pleasure of all these good people. I think you had best get in
your little car and high-tail it back to your dirty movies down
in New Orleans."

"Fuck you. You lost. Now pay up," Scud said.

"No question about it, Mr. Bellini, Matthews won according
to PAWA rules," Referee Dalton interrupted.

"I'm about tired of you, too," Bellini answered. "Charlie,
escort Mr. Dalton to his car and wish him well on his trip back
home. Scooter, ask our nigger to wait in the van."

Bellini's boys took off their jackets, revealing shoulder hol-
sters. Dalton and Big Ben Jessup left without a word of protest.

"Guns don't scare me Bellini. Give me my five grand."

No sooner were the words out of Scud's mouth than he felt
a sharp sting on the back of his leg at the knee joint. Bellini's
guard, the one with the hooded eyes, had made a small, thin cut
that barely trickled a few drops of blood.

"Just a little deeper and you'd walk in pain the rest of your
life," the guard said. "There's all kinds of ligaments, tendons,
muscles there that would give you a real nice limp."

"I want my fucking money," Scud kept on, unfazed.

The guard hit him in the head with the butt of a magnum pistol. Scud went down on one knee and felt his head open up.

"We know what they do to troublemakers in Singapore, don't we?" Bellini smiled as he took out a big wooden paddle from an attaché case. Holes were drilled in it, which imparted greater pain when slapped against bare flesh.

"You ain't using that on me," Scud mumbled as blood began to seep out of his hairline.

"Shut up!" the guard yelled and kicked him in the gut with the toe of a boot.

"Ungh!" was the sound that came out.

"I'm a believer in corporal punishment, Mr. Matthews. Nothing like a good ass-whuppin' to keep society's bad elements in line. Works in Singapore like a charm. No crime there at all. A boy can leave a bicycle in a crowded marketplace and no one will dare touch it. What do you think would happen if a boy did that here?"

"I really just don't give a shit," Scud said as he was kicked again.

"That's right, Matthews. That bicycle would be stolen about this fast," Bellini snapped his fingers for emphasis. "When they had corporal punishment in our schools, America was a safe place. A person could walk the streets without fear. Not now. The bleeding hearts made it a crime to spank an unruly child. Call it abuse. And just look at where that's got us. Scud, I think you were one of those unruly children who needed a good ass-whuppin'. I think you need a little taste of what authority and order is all about. Boys, tie Mr. Matthews to that table."

The spectators were dead silent. When Bellini stopped talking a few people took notice of a splashing, pouring sound close by. As Scud was hustled to the table at gunpoint, blood streaming down his face, the crowd, almost as one, became aware that a flow of diesel fuel had begun to wash across the parking lot. All attention immediately turned to its source.

Itch stood by a tanker truck smoking a very large cigar. He had opened a valve on the truck's tank, and diesel fuel was gushing and spreading quickly over the asphalt. He clapped his hands in applause.

"It's been real fun, and you put on one helluva show, Bellini. But unless you want to toast like a marshmallow, I suggest you drop all, and I do mean *all,* of your guns and weapons."

Itch removed the cigar from his mouth and held it over the diesel fuel.

"Do it boys. I think he means it," Bellini said, fear choking his voice.

The three guards hesitantly took out their pistols and knives and dropped them. Bellini dropped his paddle.

Scud gathered the pistols and knives and wiped his face with a towel left on the wrestling table. In a blinding motion, Scud grabbed the throat of the guard who had cut him and squeezed hard with his vice-grip fingers. He felt the guard's windpipe collapse and he let him drop to the ground, writhing in pain and surprise. Scud watched with a smile as the guard gasped unsuccessfully for air, turning blue and finally purple.

Scud turned his attention to the others. He walked behind one guard, leveled a pistol, and blew his kneecap across the parking lot. He did the same to the remaining guard.

He then picked up Bellini's paddle.

"You know Mr. Bellini, I believe in corporal punishment too. You see I had my bicycle stolen when I was a boy. And I bet it was some asshole like you that stole it. I'd say you're due for about ten good licks. Tell you what, though. I'll let you buy off some licks at, say, a thousand dollars each. How's that?"

Bellini trembled as he tried to count off five thousand dollars.

Scud grabbed the whole roll.

"Now shuck the pants off."

"C'mon Scud, I wasn't serious. I..."

Scud thumped his nose with his middle finger, not enough to do any damage, just smart like hell.

"I said shuck 'em down."

Bellini did as he was told.

"Underwear too."

He peeled down his jockey shorts.

"Bend over."

Bellini began to sob as he bent over, "Please, I..."

When wood met ass it sounded like a rifle shot. Bellini went flying across the pavement and passed out cold, face down in the diesel fuel. A huge red welt filled with pin-sized drops of blood covered both cheeks like a racing stripe.

"Get the nigger and let's get the fuck out of here," Scud told Itch.

Big Ben Jessup was even more surprised and a little scared when Itch motioned him out of the van. "Let's go," Itch said. Ben followed hesitantly.

As the three were making tracks out of the parking lot a large figure stepped out of the shadows with a smaller second figure in a wheelchair.

"Whoo-ee, that was some entertainment, Scud," Carroll Thurston said. "It's the last time anybody's going to win any money betting on you, though. How's it going, Ignatio?"

"I've had better days," Itch replied.

The three drove to a secluded area outside nearby Marion, Arkansas where a high-performance Firebird was waiting. Its windows were deeply shaded.

"Ben, take this piece-of-shit Nova and get back to New Albany as fast as you can," Itch said. "You can have it if you want it; it'll get you home anyway. One word of advice. Take back roads all the way."

"Okay," Ben answered, his head still whirling from all that had gone down.

"One more thing," Itch added. "Don't take any of this shit personally."

Chapter 11

Carroll Thurston felt as though he were swimming in a sauna. It was an August night in Memphis, and even at 1:30 in the morning it was hot and humid enough for his shirt to stick to his back. He had called Heather Madison around midnight and asked if she would meet him at the Red Lantern, an after-hours shot-and-beer joint that catered to mid-town's barflies and night prowlers. Because it stayed open until sunrise, thanks to appropriate palm greasing at the Memphis Police Department, it was a favorite hangout of bartenders, who had few places to water after closing time.

Carroll needed a drink. The PAWA World Tournament was less than a year away, in May, in St. Louis. He wanted to train and he wanted to stay focused. He didn't need women trouble. He and Heather had become tight as ticks. Even with their different work schedules they still managed to find plenty of time to spend together.

He was happy. She was happy. But Carroll couldn't shake off his feelings for Pamela McTeague. He had been with her only the one time, but there had been subsequent phone calls, letters, and postcards. It added up to something. Byron was crazy about him too, and insisted on talking to him whenever either party phoned. Carroll had spoken to Pamela about Heather and she was surprisingly understanding.

"Carroll," she had told him, "do you think I could expect you to remain uninvolved with other women when we live more than two hundred miles apart? Surely you don't expect *me* to be alone between visits?"

"No, of course not," he assured her. "It's just that most of the women I've been involved with over the years make it an all-or-nothing proposition. I'm glad you're different."

"Carroll, life's too short to be any other way."

Carroll watched as Heather parked her Volkswagen Cabriolet across the street from the Red Lantern. She skipped across the avenue, hugged him tightly, and gave him a kiss as warm and wet as the Memphis night. When they opened the door to the bar they were met with an arctic blast of cold air. The Red Lantern could be counted on for two things: sub-zero air-conditioning and sub-zero beer. Heather had brought a sweater just in case. She immediately slipped into it.

There were a good dozen people in the Red Lantern. Two skinny redneck boys with long, stringy hair and nicotine-stained fingers hovered over the rickety pool table. One older patron pumped quarters into the video poker machine, a gambling device long outlawed in Memphis, but openly displayed at the Red Lantern. The rest sat at the bar, talking quietly and drinking. Ray Charles's "Mess Around" throbbed out of the jukebox.

"Honey, you sounded so serious on the phone," Heather said as they sat at a small table. "Is anything the matter?"

"No, not really. I just wanted to talk," Carroll said. "I've been doing a lot of thinking about us, how much I like you, like being around you..."

"You're not going to ask me to marry you, are you?" Heather laughed slyly. "I expect better than the Red Lantern, sweetheart."

Carroll laughed. "Hmm, I hadn't thought of that, but now that you mention it, Heather, will you...uh, will you...split a pitcher of beer with me?"

They both laughed.

"Uh-uh," Heather said, "You have to get my father's permission first."

At that moment the door to the Red Lantern flew open and a slight, dapper man wearing Buddy Holly-style glasses and slicked-back hair staggered in. There was an audible groan at the bar and Carroll joined in the chorus.

"Who is that?" Heather asked.

"Lambert Higginbotham," Carroll answered.

"The photographer?"

"Yeah. Part-time genius. Full-time stumblebum."

Higginbotham parked himself at the table in the farthest corner of the bar. Even though it was blistering hot outside, Higginbotham wore jodphurs and riding boots, a wool vest, and a tweed jacket. He looked like slightly addled British gentry and was known as one of Memphis's most troublesome drunks, a dangerous alcoholic who owned too many expensive handguns for his own good. In particular, he liked to show off a Nazi-era Luger imprinted with a swastika.

Higginbotham hollered, "Service goddammit!" He mumbled to himself, then began to kick the wall with his boot.

Katy, the owner of the Red Lantern, scurried over with two shots of bourbon and a beer, his standing order. "Lambert, you hush now. You're disturbing customers. You know you always get looked after, so just hush and calm down."

"Calm down?" he slurred. "How can I calm down when I don't have a goddamn thing to drink? Tha's gra'tude for ya." His face bobbed towards the shot glass.

❖ ❖ ❖

"I can't stand that guy," Carroll said. "We have to kick him out of The Bombay two or three times a month."

"Don't pay him any attention hon," Heather said. "Anything else you wanted to tell me?"

"Heather, there's somebody else."

There was an uncomfortable pause.

"Somebody else? What do you mean?" She looked like she had been slapped.

"I care too much for you to lie to you or sneak around behind your back. Heather, I think I might love you, but I want you to know about another woman who lives in Nashville."

"Oh, I get it. She's the *real* reason you went to Nashville when you went to the Special Olympics," she snapped.

"No, no, Heather. I met this little boy who has Down's syndrome at the Olympics, and she's his mother. We met that day by accident, and we just hit it off. I've only been with her that once. But we've stayed in touch. I didn't want to cover up anything and I wanted to lay it out straight for you. We're too involved for me to be keeping secrets."

Lambert Higginbotham momentarily interrupted their discussion when he yelled out, "Katy, bring me a goddamn cheeseburger, with everything on it." He snapped his fingers, as if to speed up his order.

"Carroll, do you love her?" Heather asked through tears.

"I don't know yet. I do care about her though."

"What does she look like?"

Carroll described Pamela as objectively as he could.

"She's not as pretty as me, is she?" Heather huffed.

"Not in the conventional sense, no."

Heather didn't like his answer. Carroll could see the Sicilian in her blood beginning to rise.

"Just tell me one thing," Heather fired back. "Did you sleep with her?"

"Well, in a manner of speaking."

"You bastard!" she shrieked. She picked up her beer and threw it into his face where the cold hit him like a doubled-up fist. After grabbing her handbag, she ran out the door squalling.

Carroll sat there stunned and drenched. The folks at the bar stared for a moment and went back to their drinks.

"Goddammit you know I don't like may'naise," Higginbotham snarled as he sailed his cheeseburger and plate across the room. The plate struck a picture just behind Carroll's head, knocking it to the floor. A hundred or so cockroaches that had been huddled for warmth behind the picture scattered in every direction.

At first sight of the roaches, men and women screamed for mercy and scrambled on top of the bar, tables, chairs, and even the jukebox. The two redneck boys at the pool table began to flail away at the roaches with their pool sticks. Katy—who was apparently used to crawling things in her bar—calmy flattened a dozen or so with a flyswatter. Within a couple of minutes the surviving roaches had found new hiding places, and the Red Lantern went on, business as usual.

Carroll, who hadn't moved a muscle the whole time, found himself laughing despite being soaked by beer and stung by Heather's fury. Just wait until the PAWA Tournament, he thought to himself.

"Get me another fucking burger you fucking bitch," Lambert Higginbotham went on, unfazed by the commotion.

Carroll Thurston got up, went over to Higginbotham, and grabbed his belt at the seat of his pants.

"I've had about enough of your rummy ass," Carroll spoke

with a voice like doom. He bounced him to the front door, Higginbotham's arms waving wildly, and heaved him into the middle of the street.

When he walked back to his table Katy fixed him with a hard look that let him know she was in a state of high piss-off and said, "I hope you know that was my best customer."

Chapter 12

"This man, born Stephen Strawn in the small rural community of Ripley, Tennessee over forty years ago, took the lowly sport of arm wrestling—long considered the province of rednecks and toughs in out-of-the-way bars and liquor joints—to new heights, enjoyed by millions of sports enthusiasts on programs such as ABC's *Wide World of Sports*," intoned America's best-known television journalist. "In the process, Steve Strawn became a larger-than-life-personality who eventually changed his name to Steve Strong, and thus became a household word. Immortalized by artist Andy Warhol, whose portrait of Strong's massive, muscular arm today hangs in the Museum of Modern Art, Steve Strong ten years ago was one of America's most visible and celebrated figures.

"But where, you might ask, is Steve Strong today?

"Six months ago *Sixty Minutes* found Steve Strong in this Nashville hospital, according to doctors only one step away from death's door. The reason behind the illness of a man once celebrated as the health icon of millions around the world?"

The camera cut to Steve Strong, who almost looked the picture of his former health.

"Anabolic steroids," answered Steve Strong on camera. "Six months ago I was as addicted to anabolic steroids as any crackhead on the streets of New York City is to crack cocaine. I couldn't get up in the morning without a steroid fix. I couldn't go to sleep without juicing. At any one time, I might have been using up to twelve different steroid medications, not to mention all the other drugs."

The journalist narrowed his eyes and asked in his familiar confrontational tone, "Steve, why in God's name would a superb athlete such as yourself, beloved by millions, a man at the pinnacle of his profession, a man who seemingly had it all, jeopardize everything he stood for by allowing a senseless addiction like this?"

Steve appeared thoughtful. "Mike, I would have done anything, and I do mean *anything*, to have an edge over my competition. For a long time I had pretty well trashed all comers to the sport. I dominated arm wrestling for nearly two decades. But some of the newer guys who had watched me from the sidelines began to imitate my tactics and my style. Some of these guys were not only like forces of nature at the arm wrestling table— they were just that strong—but they had the smarts too. To put 'em down I needed not only an edge, I needed *every* edge."

The journalist took a couple of eight-by-ten glossy photographs out of an envelope.

"Steve, do you remember these?" the journalist asked.

The camera cut to the photos which showed a man whose face had been beaten into a purple mask. One eye was completely closed shut and the other was streaked with blood.

"Unfortunately, yes," Steve soberly replied. "This was just one example of my 'roid rages."

"'Roid rages?" the journalist asked.

"Prolonged use of steroids can bring about uncontrollable

rages that can be triggered by just about anything. Insiders call them 'roid rages. This man was a waiter whose service wasn't fast enough to suit me at this particular moment on this particular day. Thirty minutes earlier and I may not have even noticed him. But one spark at the wrong time and the 'roids just took over."

"I understand he's suing you now. For how much money?"

"Two million dollars for starters. I can't say I blame him. My lawyer told me not to talk about it, but what's not to know? I went crazy on steroids and beat the man half to death. If you're watching this, man, I want to say I'm sorry. I was out of my head, and if I had been in control it never would have happened."

"Steve, what made you decide to finally kick the steroid habit?"

"A dozen kidney stones will clear your mind real fast, Mike. I've dealt with pain my whole professional life, but with twelve kidney stones you're talking *pain*. But the real reason I put 'em down for good is that I came *this* close to stomping the crap out of a troop of Girl Scouts who came to my door selling Girl Scout cookies. It was like something inside whispered, 'that's enough.'"

❖ ❖ ❖

The *Sixty Minutes* team revisited the scene of Steve Strong's near death, intercutting interviews with the paramedics, doctors, old gym buddies, and family members with the audio tape of his desperate 911 call.

The next scene cut to Steve Strong happily munching a Girl Scout Do-Si-Do cookie.

"And how is Steve Strong today after years of ultimately debilitating steroid use?" asked the journalist.

"I intend on winning the PAWA World Tournament," Strong replied to the off-camera interviewer. "I feel better today than I've felt in ten, maybe even fifteen years. The arm strength is back, no loss there at all. My workouts have been the most focused and productive of my career. My reflexes need a little work, but even that is progressing faster than I could have ever imagined."

As if to prove him right, the camera crew went inside his home, showing Steve Strong red-faced and straining, sweat pouring in rivulets down his face, doing a battery of exercises with his robotics. The camera then cut to Steve Strong red-faced and straining in a completely different environment, in a hospital undergoing leg exercises with a physical therapist.

"At this stage, the only apparent permanent damage done to Steve Strong that he must contend with on a day-to-day basis is an almost crippling degeneration of his knee joints, which, according to one of his orthopedic surgeons, were, quote, the consistency of Elmer's Glue, unquote. Extensive invasive surgery and the insertion of plastic plates have restored movement and taken away the chronic pain. But, doctors have told him, he will never again have full ambulatory ability. Today Steve Strong must walk slowly and carefully with the aid of a walking cane."

The camera panned to Steve Strong, who walked not unlike a geriatric patient, feeling his way down the sidewalk to his home.

"If I were involved in any other sport besides arm wrestling, I'd be finished, *finito*, another wash-out. In other sports, you see, the legs are critical to athletic performance. Take boxing, for instance. When the legs go a boxer has no way to absorb the shock of a punch. And he can't move fast enough to avoid his opponent. Arm wrestling, however, is nearly all upper body. Anyone can make strength gains in his—or her—arm and wrist muscles up to nearly retirement age." Steve Strong flashed his million dollar smile, "And this year, I plan on making a few gains myself."

The camera cut away to the familiar ticking stop-watch.

In the next months, Steve Strong became the centerpiece of a *cause célèbre*, appearing on *Montel Williams, Regis and Kathie*

Lee, and *Geraldo*, always introduced as he slowly and dramatically made his entrance through the studio audience, walking with the help of a cane. He lectured on the horrors of steriod abuse at college campuses and medical symposiums, before Congress, the President's Council on Physical Fitness, and MTV.

It was good to be back.

Chapter 13

Carroll Thurston sat under four hundred seventy pounds of cold steel, the muscles in his chest and arms burning like they were being basted on a spit. Barry Daniels sat in his wheelchair at the head of the weight bench, spotting for Carroll.

"You're loaded up too heavy," said Barry. "You only got four reps out of that set. You need to lighten up."

"No, man," Carroll said between gasps for air. "This is intentional. It's my system. I'm ready for another set."

Carroll gripped the weight bar tightly. He had sanded the knurled grips on the bar smooth, forcing him to fight harder for a good grip, the better to add power to his wrist and fingers. With Barry's help he brought the four hundred seventy pounds down slowly to his nipple line. He clenched his jaws and began to exhale and push, until his arms were straight out, then he steadily lowered the bar back to his chest. His face was a crimson burn and veins jolted out from his neck and forehead. He screamed through the final two reps.

"Okay. Let's take off a hundred pounds."

After resting his muscles for a few minutes, Carroll began to work the reduced load. He got only three reps out of the set before collapsing.

"Take off another hundred."

He repeated the steps until his muscles were so drained and wasted he could barely bring his water bottle to his mouth.

Barry shook his head, disbelieving. "How can you hope to build mass when you're not getting in any reps? I've been getting in twenty or more reps each set and it works great for me."

"Yeah, look at you," Carroll responded flatly. "You're a splendid physical specimen all right. I bet all the juice jockeys at the gym love the cut of your bi's, pecs, and lats. But we're not after looks here, Barry. We're after strength. I'm stressing each muscle to its full capacity; now I'll wait a full four days for healing and strength gain before lifting again. I'll do some running for stamina, a lot of reflex exercises for speed, and some light stretches to keep the muscles warm and lubricated. But that's basically it for power building for at least four more days. I'll soak in a hot Jacuzzi once or twice a day, and I'll go to the gym to get a good rubdown when I'm really sore, but that's it. Believe me though, Barry, this system pays off. Now let's do some curls with the butterfly attachment."

The master bedroom in Carroll's midtown Memphis home had been converted into a training room filled with racks of weights, pulleys, benches, and a stand-up arm wrestling table. A framed reproduction of Andy Warhol's *The Man With the Golden Arm* portrait of Steve Strong's arm hung on one wall and was the room's only decorating touch. The remainder of the house was a generic bachelor's pad, with a wide screen TV, expensive stereo, and dirty dishes in the sink.

Carroll inserted an odd-shaped contraption into the weight rack.

"What the hell is that?" asked Barry.

"A homemade rig. My custom butterfly attachment. I've added on some steel pipes bent out and flared to fit my full range of motion. By using this and lifting with my palms flat up, my wrists and forearms get just as much workout as the pecs. The hand and wrist are everything to a puller, but all the muscle groups have to learn to work together. There are eighteen muscles in the forearm alone. Depending on the pull, one wrestler may play off your forearm muscles, another may be all wrist and fingers then switch to power down from his shoulder. That's why the muscles have to learn to love each other. They have to be hardwired together into a solid, deadly unit."

It took several adjustments for the weight equipment to work properly and smoothly for Barry. Using his massive upper body, he was able to swing from his wheelchair to the weight benches with relative ease. His spindly, atrophied legs dangled uselessly behind, and occasionally he picked them up with his hands and gently positioned them out of harm's way.

Barry was a monster with the weights, however, and although he had a much smaller body frame than Carroll, he could lift nearly the same loads. He was clearly uncomfortable working with the higher weights and lower reps, but Barry had heart and gave every ounce to it.

"Jeez, this is a killer workout," panted Barry when he was through. "You really think it'll do me any good for the type of wheelchair racing I'm doing?"

"No doubt about it," answered Carroll. "You need all the upper body power you can get, and this is the best way I've found to do it. You haven't been doing anything special for your wrist and fingers either, but a solid power grip on the wheel rim is bound to give you a hell of an edge."

"What do you suggest, coach?"

"Let me show you a top secret technique of mine." Carroll motioned for him to follow, and they moved from the house to the back yard. Carroll picked up a long-handled snow shovel with a heavy scoop on the end that was resting against a wood fence. Carroll gripped the end of the shovel handle and extended the shovel and his right arm out as far as he could. Using only the muscles in his wrist and fingers, he began to work the shovel up and down.

Barry Daniels didn't seem particularly impressed.

"It doesn't look like much," conceded Carroll, "but very few average Joes can get the shovel pan off the ground. Here, try it."

Barry took the shovel, extended it as far from his right side as possible, then fully extended his right arm so that the shovel pan rested a good six or seven feet away. He lifted it off the ground and immediately understood Carroll's meaning. The exercise was deceptive. It was, in fact, a real ball-buster and was bound to firm up a weak grip. Or make a crusher grip out of one that was already strong.

"Twenty minutes with that on your weight training days will amaze you. You already know about my chair workouts, like what I did over at the Peabody Hotel. I take turns, one training day with the chairs, one training day with the shovel. They work."

Barry waited at the bottom of the long hill for Carroll's signal. They had driven in Barry's van over to the long slope on Dwight Road in the old Charjean community. Although the neighborhood had once been an unremarkable blue-collar enclave for Christian fundamentalists, they had long since fled to even less remarkable suburbs, leaving Charjean to poor blacks. Barry had become something of a neighborhood fixture, his wheelchair training and sleek racing chair objects of great curiosity, especially to the children who invariably gathered to watch.

"Go!" Carroll motioned and shouted as he simultaneously began a countdown on a stopwatch.

Isolating the moment in his mind, Barry pumped furiously at the thin, high-pressure tires on his modified wheelchair. The cheering of the children along the sidewalk, "C'mon Barrah," "Go, champ," never got past his ears. All he could think was stroke, stroke, stroke. The hundred meters to the top could have been a hundred miles.

"Twenty-four point three seconds," said Carroll as Barry braked his chair and bent double, trying to catch his breath.

"Not bad, not bad," Barry wheezed as he swished water in his mouth and spit. "Let's do it again."

Barry popped a wheelie and flew to the bottom of the hill, causing the children to clap and holler.

He signalled to Carroll that he was ready.

"Go!" yelled Carroll as he clicked the stopwatch.

Barry threw down hard on his wheel rim, off to a tremendous start. He was at least at his personal best, he felt it, knew it in the way professional athletes can sense in their bones they're pushing beyond their envelope.

The right tire picked up a slender, sharp sliver of glass from the pavement that neatly sliced through the leather in his glove and stabbed Barry in a sensitive spot on his palm, causing his downstroke to break unevenly. The chair quickly lost balance and within a split second Barry and the chair flipped and rolled several turns across the hot asphalt.

Carroll ran as fast as he could over to Barry, who was moving but groggy and severely scraped. His jogging outfit was badly torn and the urine bag tucked away inside his pants had come undone and was lying near a gutter grate. The neighborhood children gaped at it.

"Barry, are you okay?" Carroll pleaded.

"Not really," he answered as he drew himself together. "Whew, I've got some nasty road rashes. I better check and see if there's any damage below the waist. Give me a hand with the shoes and pants legs."

Carroll took off the shoes and socks and helped Barry peel out of his jogging pants as he sat on the scalding asphalt. He had two particularly vicious scrapes along one leg, one of which had opened enough to require stitches. The children

murmured a collective "ooh" when they caught sight of the
blood. The end of the catheter that connected to Barry's urine
bag trailed out embarrassingly from his jockey shorts.

As Barry wiped the gravel from his scrapes he noticed Carroll
was very quiet. He glanced at him and saw that Carroll was
weaving, his face drained of color.

"Sit down, man! You're about to pass out."

Carroll sat down on the curb as ordered and put his head
between his knees. He fought down the vomit that had risen in
his throat. A small black boy silently brought him Barry's water
bottle.

Another boy brought the urine bag to Barry, who attached it
and pulled on his pants.

"Is 'at pee in dat bag?"

"Yeah. Thanks for bringing it, podna."

"Why you gotta pee in a bag?"

"I can't stand up on my legs to pee like you can, so I gotta
pee somewhere. It's a lot easier to just pee in a bag and empty
it out when I'm good and ready."

Carroll was still shaken after they had gone to the minor
emergency clinic and Barry had received six stitches to close the
gash in his leg.

"It's okay, Carroll. Remember, I don't feel a thing in those
legs. It's no big deal, no bones were broken. I've flipped before."

"I'm sorry, Barry. I don't know what happened out there.
Man, I've seen blood and guts and broken arms ever since I've
been pulling, but today it all just hit me differently. I'm
ashamed of myself. You're the one scraped all to hell and I'm
the one fainting like a goddamn schoolgirl. Weird."

"Carroll, can I ask you a personal question?"

"Sure."

"You have a hard time around handicapped people, don't you?"

"What do you mean?"

"I watched you at the Special Olympics in Nashville before I spoke to you. It took you a long time to warm to the task. When we were in high school I always felt you were a little bit afraid of my handicap. It was like you were worried something out of the ordinary could happen at any time when you were around me. You seemed uncomfortable with it all. In all honesty, you still do."

"You've got it partly right," Carroll answered after a moment's pause. "The truth is, you were always something of an inspiration to me. You had the courage and grit to overcome a lot of shitty circumstances, and I admired that, that drive and determination and desire to achieve. You left a deep impression, whether you knew it or not. You weren't one of those self-pitying jackasses who wants to change the order of the universe to accommodate the needs of the handicapped. You just chomped down and changed yourself.

"That's why I wanted to work out with you. You spur me on and make me reach inside to give all I've got. You bring out the best in me.

"But to answer your question, yeah, to be honest I've always been a little freaked by handicapped people. A phobia, I guess. You know, when I was little, I didn't much have the heart for sports, even though I was a lot stronger than other kids my age. I was in the Cub Scouts about this same time. Mom was the Den Mother, which meant we had a gang of scouts over at the house once a week. One of our projects was to make little favors for the kids at the Crippled Children's Home that used to be out Lamar Avenue close to the Katz Drug Store. It's been closed for years now."

"I remember the place," Barry said. "The red-brick one-story building that had a long circular drive and landscaped grounds."

"That's it. Well, my mother was volunteered into delivering these favors out to the home. So a couple of other Cub Scouts and I put on our uniforms, loaded the favors in the back seat of our car, and Mom drove us over. When we first walked in we were told to wait in the lobby for the Director. About the time we were seated good, they wheeled out a girl in a bed—at least I think it was a bed—that looked like it had been built in Frankenstein's laboratory.

"In those days really sick kids were put in institutions—out of sight, out of mind. Hell, Barry, you probably know a lot more about this shit than I do. All I can say is what we saw there scared the daylights out of us. Kids in iron lungs, upside down on rotating platforms. It's a terrible thing to look and see pain in another child's face.

"When I first went into the home I could see this kid—a boy maybe six or seven years old—way off down a connecting hallway. He had braces on every limb of his body including a huge padded one around his head and neck. But I could see his face. I still see his face. He was smiling at me like he wanted to play. He was standing all by himself in the middle of this long hallway and he started walking towards me. He had all those braces moving and making this ungodly clanking noise. He moved maybe six inches at a time.

"I was a scared, dumb kid and went about my business as fast as I could carrying the favors back and forth into the Director's office. Every time I glanced at this little boy, he was a foot or two closer. Then he tried to speak to me, but the words came out all garbled like an old Victrola record winding down.

"You know, I bet not a month goes by that I don't dream about that kid," he went on. "It scared me then and it still scares me, at least when I dream about it. That's the story. I guess that's why I get a little freaked sometimes around handicapped people. Not all of 'em, of course. But yeah, you're right. I guess I do have a problem."

"What year would all this have been?" asked Barry.

"1967 or so," said Carroll.

"Hmm," said Barry as he wheeled his van into the post office parking lot.

"Hope you don't mind me stopping at the post office," said Barry. "I haven't picked up the mail at my P.O. box in a couple of weeks."

"Not at all," said Carroll.

The parking lot was packed, and just as Barry was signalling to turn into the only available handicapped spot a teenager in an open air Jeep whipped into the opening.

Carroll felt his hackles rise.

They watched in seething anger as the pimple-faced boy leapt out of the vehicle and bounded inside the post office.

"God, that just about burns my ass up," said Carroll.

"I've got ways of getting even," Barry smiled wickedly.

He pulled in directly behind the Jeep, blocking it from any possibility of an exit. Barry reached into his back seat and retrieved an old pump-type oil can with a flexible spout. He got out of the van, rolled up to the Jeep, and squirted a single brown stream of oil across the windshield.

Then Barry went in to pick up his mail.

The boy stared at his feet as he shuffled to his Jeep and was opening the door before he noticed he had been blocked in. He wore baggy pants that exposed at least six inches of boxer shorts and a T-shirt that had the logo of the Dayglo Abortions, a punk rock group, on it. Below the logo was a cartoon of Ronald and Nancy Reagan sporting vampire fangs, sitting down to a plate of aborted fetuses. The boy's hair was shaved completely bald on the sides with a long plume of hair in the front that hung nearly to his chin. He had to sling the hair out of his eyes in order to see.

"Motherfucker!" the boy said to himself. Then he noticed Carroll sitting on the shotgun side of the van.

"Hey man, would you mind, like, moving your fucking van?"

"It's not my van."

"I don't really give a rat's ass whose van it is. Just move the motherfucker."

Barry rolled up behind the boy.

"Listen you little snot-nosed shit," said Barry. "Don't you know it's against the law to park in a handicapped spot without a sticker? I don't see a sticker on your Jeep"

"Who gives a fuck? Just move the fucking van?"

"I will when I've gone through all my mail." Barry held up a thick stack.

"The fuck you will. I said move it, *now!*" The kid shoved the wheelchair almost knocking Barry out of it for the second time that day.

Before Carroll could jump out of the van to help, Barry had taken out a telescoping baton he kept in his chair to ward off bad dogs and brought it down savagely across the boy's calf. The boy went down instantly.

Barry held the baton over the boy as he cringed in fear and pain.

"I want you to get a little taste of what it's like to fight a handicap, you spoiled little prick." He brought the baton down again, bringing a howl of pain from the boy.

"Get up and walk to the front door, then I'll let you out."

With tears streaming down his cheeks, the boy tried to regain his footing. He could barely stand on his injured leg, but with the baton waving only inches away he hobbled, hopped, and stumbled to the front door of the post office and dragged himself crying back to his Jeep.

"Apologize to him," ordered Carroll, who brought himself to his full height and leaned into the Jeep's window.

"I apologize," he said.

"You can do better than that, asshole," warned Carroll.

"I apologize, *man*," he implored.

"Didn't your parents teach you to say 'sir'?"

"I apologize, *sir*," he wept.

The small crowd that had gathered cheered and whistled.

It was two days later before the boy took notice of the brown streak on his window and turned on his washer/wipers. The whole windshield turned into an ugly, oily smear and the boy spent the better part of half an hour wiping it clean with his Dayglo Abortions T-shirt.

Chapter 14

Carroll had noticed the tall, slender brunette the minute she walked into The Bombay Bar. He could tell from her tentativeness that it was the first time she had set foot in the place. She was conservatively dressed in a smart glen-plaid suit with a lavender blouse buttoned to the neck with a finely etched cameo resting at the collar.

This woman, whoever she was, had a stunning, flawless peaches-and-cream complexion with long, curling eyelashes and full pouting lips. She was definitely a major league babe, a babe with more curves than a Grand Prix raceway.

Although Carroll was still fighting his hurt from Heather's unexpected flight from the Red Lantern Lounge, looking at this gorgeous woman could not help but make his pulse dance.

"I *know* I can help you," he smiled stupidly as he placed a napkin in front of her.

She gave him one of those smarmy, withering looks that was half back-off and half come-on.

"I'll have a sloe gin fizz, please, if it's not too much trouble," she said, revealing teeth as white as bleached ivory.

"Ma'am, nothing would be too much trouble for you. A sloe gin fizz it is then."

It had been four weeks since Heather had thrown the beer in his face, and she had refused to answer either her phone or door since. Incommunicado. Carroll didn't give up easily—it wasn't in him—but he had to admit Heather just about had him whipped. A month ago he would not have looked twice at this woman—well, maybe twice—but now he was practically panting after her.

"Here you are, ma'am," he said politely as he placed her drink on the tiny napkin.

"Thank you," she said and took a sip.

"How is it?" Carroll asked.

"Fine," she answered with the touch of a smile. "Are you always this interested in your bartending skills?"

"Oh yeah. Always," he answered with a sloppy grin.

"Memphis has some of the boniest men I've ever seen. How did you get so much meat on your bones?" she asked.

"Grocery power, sweetheart," he said, "plus barbecue ribs from the Rendezvous at least once a week."

"I ate at the Rendezvous yesterday. The ribs were delicious. If I lived in Memphis, I'd weigh three hundred pounds. But that's not fat hanging off your bones, honey, those are muscles. *Big* muscles. You lift weights or something?"

Jay, a college student who often worked behind the bar helping Carroll, overheard the conversation and butted in at the appropriate moment. "Lady, you're looking at Carroll Thurston, world champion arm wrestler. King Kong couldn't put this gorilla down." He slapped Carroll on the back jovially.

"Thanks, pal," Carroll said.

"A champion arm wrestler? Well, that explains the muscles. I guess you're a real tough guy, huh? A man's man?"

"No, I'm one of those warm and fuzzy cuddly assholes like

Phil Donahue and Alan Alda. All for women's rights and all that shit. And I might add you sound very bright and observant for a woman." He hesitated just long enough to make sure she knew he was putting her on.

"For a woman!" she said, acting indignant and coy at the same time. She was playing along.

"I take it you're not from Memphis?"

"No, it's my first visit. I even went to Elvis's grave. It was very, um, enlightening. His fans are an interesting group of people."

"Oh, the Elvi. Yeah, the green pedal pushers are a dead give-away."

"Is it true they arrest people at Graceland if they mention Elvis using drugs?"

"No, but they'll snatch you out of there in a New York minute. Don't want nobody speakin' ill of the King. Truth is some of those Elvi save money for years to make a pilgrimage to Graceland. Most of them are poor white trash who make little of nothing, but they are Graceland's bread and butter. The Graceland brass won't stand for wise-ass big city folks upsetting the Elvi by making drug jokes or rude comments about the tacky furniture."

"He's almost like a god to those people, isn't he?"

"*Almost* nothing. Half of 'em pray to Elvis and the other half ask God to pass along a message."

"In New Orleans we have our witch queens and reverend mothers, but nothing as weird as what goes on down at Graceland. It's intense. Even I started crying at the grave."

"So you're from New Orleans, huh? What line of work you in?"

"I'm in Product Development with Bridgewell Industries, which is headquartered in Memphis. I'm out of the New Orleans office. We market several lines of cosmetics to an African-American demographic. Most people apparently don't realize Memphis is a world center for cosmetics and beauty care products for African-Americans."

"Nope, I never knew that."

"It's Memphis's best kept secret, darlin'."

"So what brings your lovely self to our bar?"

"Well, it's been a long day at Bridgewell, and I needed something wet and tangy to relax me. I walked over from the Magnolia Inn down the block."

"Why didn't you just go to the Magnolia Inn lounge for a drink and soak up a little Memphis jazz?"

"Honey, I get enough jazz down home. Memphis jazz just doesn't blow as hot. Now Memphis *blues* on the other hand..."

"Ah, you like our blues?"

"You all got some pickers all right. My daddy used to play Albert King and B.B. King at the house all the time. I love it when B.B. gets Lucille to talkin'."

She laughed.

"Let me formally introduce myself, if I may," Carroll said. "As Jay told you, I'm Carroll Thurston, Memphis's greatest bartender, world champion arm wrestler, champion rib eater, and olympic-class nice guy. And you are...?"

"Paula Shay, but my friends call me Sugar."

"Sugar Shay, it is indeed a pleasure." He held out his hand to shake and when she extended hers he brought it to his lips and kissed it.

"Ooh, how gal-*lant*," she said.

"Miss Shay, would you allow me the privilege of making you my special drink, the Arm Twister? It's my own secret recipe. If you like Brandy Alexanders, you'll love the Arm Twister. Of course the drink is on me."

Jay overheard the offer, and right on cue said, "Wow! You're making an Arm Twister? You haven't made an Arm Twister in months. Ma'am I hope you realize what this means. Very few people receive this honor. It's better than the key to the city."

"You've sold me, baby," she laughed. "I'd be delighted, provided one of you handsome fellas walks me back to the Magnolia Inn. I'm in a strange city and I wouldn't want anyone taking advantage of a tipsy lady."

Jay jumped at the offer. "I'll be glad to walk you…"

"Like hell you will," Carroll glared at him.

"Okay, okay. You win, big guy." Jay threw up his arms in a gesture of surrender.

"Now, now boys. No roughhousing on my account," Sugar said sweetly.

"Let me fix you that drink," Carroll said.

He mixed a little half-and-half with coffee, Kahlua, Bailey's Irish Cream, and three or four other ingredients. He put it all in a blender, fizzed it a few times, and poured the frothing liquid into a small tulip-shaped glass.

"Uhmmm," she said licking her lips after a tiny sip. "Kind of like Jamoca Almond Fudge ice cream, only yummier. It's wonderful, Carroll."

"And there's not a calorie in it," Carroll said.

"Uh-huh, right," she said.

When they left The Bombay, Sugar Shay entwined her arm around Carroll's, just another lady walking with her gentleman.

"My, those arms are as solid as cypress stumps. You wouldn't hurt a fragile thing like me with those big things would you?"

"Not a chance, babe," he answered.

"So, Carroll, have you been a bartender all your life?"

"No, I was an ad copywriter most of my adult life. 'Til I got sick of all the assholes in the business. So I busted out and got a life, a poorer life sometimes, but a life nonetheless. How about you?"

"Oh, I've been in the fashion and cosmetics industry for some time. I was a scholarship student at Tulane, where I majored in Marketing, specializing in the fashion trade. You may have noticed I'm rather tall for a woman."

"Yes, I noticed lots of things about you."

She cleared her throat. "Ahem, well I was a women's basketball player also."

"I thought you had the look of an athlete."

They entered the lobby, rode the elevator to the third floor, and Carroll escorted Sugar Shay to her door.

"Carroll, it was nice to meet you. Thanks for the Arm Twister. You've really made this trip special."

"Can I see you tomorrow, Sugar?" Carroll asked.

"That's sweet, Carroll, but I fly back at ten tomorrow morning."

"Dang, just my luck."

"I've got to go," she said softly, invitingly.

Carroll slowly leaned over and saw her lips part. He drank her in like cool water. Their lips separated and they eased apart looking deep into one another's eyes. She held her room key out at arm's length and let it drop to the floor.

Carroll picked it up, unlocked the door, and they both went for each other the second the door was closed behind them, swimming in warm lips and saliva.

She excused herself to the bathroom for a minute and came back nearly undressed. Carroll delicately slid off her tiny red panties, revealing an ass laid out like a Honeybaked Ham. The symmetry of her cheeks would have made a Greek sculptor weep for joy.

Carroll carefully parted her thighs and noticed that the sweet groove had been slathered with a lotion slipperier than a quart of Slick 50. She was prepped and waiting.

He moved up on her with great care and ease. After all, he made at least two of her. She reached to him with her long, thin fingers and expertly snaked him into her. He felt the warm lotion lap onto him and he entered her as smoothly as a prow through stilled waters. He gingerly began to thrust deeper and deeper and Sugar arched her back to meet him.

They operated like a perfect tongue-and-groove, and after several minutes of furious lovemaking, Carroll exploded into her, mixing sex fluids with the synthetic, viscous ones she had pre-applied. Both of their chests heaved from exhaustion. Carroll rolled off of her and pulled her on top. He kissed her slowly and deliberately and dipped one hand back to plumb the dark recesses of her ass.

After several more minutes she cooed in his ear, "I'm a little gooey. I think I'll wash up and slip into my pajamas. Carroll, hon, you're going to need to leave now, so I can get some rest for tomorrow. You've been very sweet, and a very good lover. If I'm in Memphis again..."

He smiled and leaned in to kiss her. She didn't need to say another word.

Sugar darted out of the bed like a cat, waved goodbye, and disappeared into the bathroom where Carroll could hear running water as he dressed. After smoothing the wrinkles in his clothes and raking his fingers through his hair, he started to walk out of the room when he noticed what appeared to be a sprig of mistletoe taped over the door. He reached his hand to touch the plant, but then thought better of it and instead stood on his tiptoes to sniff it. It gave off a wild, biting odor that he couldn't place. It definitely wasn't mistletoe. With a look of puzzlement on his face, Carroll adjusted his balls, hiked up his britches, and quietly closed the door behind him.

Carroll was awakened at nine o'clock sharp the next morning by a driver from the Acadiana Seafood Collective who delivered a large container of live bluepoint crabs. A card inside read, "Hope you enjoy them, Kisses, Scud Matthews."

Immediately suspicious that Scud was up to no good, Carroll called The Bombay's head chef who assured him that a live crab was, in all probability, a healthy crab, that there was little like-lihood of tampering. The chef encouraged Carroll to bring the crabs to the kitchen at once so they could be prepared and eaten before they started dying, which was inevitable within a matter of hours.

A good dozen people at The Bombay devoured the crabs with great relish, and Carroll had to admit they were good. *Too* good. He couldn't help but wonder what Scud was trying to prove. This wasn't just some friendly gesture.

A few nights later Carroll kept waking to an intense itching in his crotch. It finally got bad enough that he had to get up and turn on the lights.

"Crabs!" he moaned.

Then he got it. Some fucking joke. Sugar indeed.

Chapter 15

Eight-point-one percent. To the layman, eight-point-one percent wouldn't mean dick, but Steve Strong knew it was enough to murder him at the wrestling table. It had been eight years since Steve Strong pulled his personal best. He was into full-blown steroid jacking by then, but that was long before the downside dragged him into a deep, dark hole. At the last PAWA World Tournament, which was held four years ago, the same year as the Olympics, Steve was down nine-point-seven percent, and he was blown out of the competition before he had broken a decent sweat. He left the tournament so fast and quietly that many of the athletes thought he was a no-show. They could not have known he was a dying man.

But Steve Strong was back, almost good as new. His knees—well, that was another story for another day. Otherwise, he felt great; he could sleep eight hours straight, could eat a solid meal and keep it down, and even his plumbing was in reasonable working order. He could also get it up again and wasted no time in proving it. The tabloids were all over the Steve Strong saga and smacked their lips over every celebrity and starlet who whispered in his ear. Steve loved it.

But the damn eight-point-one percent loss was serious. Winning meant everything, especially now. He had gotten a taste of what it was like to be a has-been and it had been a bitter fruit. The doors stopped opening, the phones stopped ringing, the legs stopped spreading. He might as well have been dead.

Now Steve Strong concentrated his whole life on his upper body. In the past he had done five miles of roadwork a day, really as more of a morning wakeup than anything. You didn't need long wind in the sport of arm wrestling. Many pulls were so fast you literally could not blink, or you'd miss it all. Five miles would burn off every speck of fat you could eat, it was true. But arm wrestling was a sport in which washtub-sized guts were the norm. Looking lean and ripped was purely an act of vanity.

So, Steve Strong spent his days in workout. The robotics took him through a battery of reflex and strength tests, covering practically every muscle and digit of significance above the waist. Steve still preferred gym workouts when it came to the heavy weights, however. Pumping iron twice a week was almost a ritual, a communal experience, for Steve. The solitude of his home workouts was leavened by the male-bonding aspects of pumping in public, with old buddies shouting encouragement and patting him on the back when the show of strength was spectacular. The smell of the locker room alone was enough to get his blood singing.

At times, when the 'roids had been raging, he would dare people to look at him when he was pumping. He kept a wet rag close at hand to throw at those who stared a little too long. The "splat!" sound of a soaked towel slapping someone upside the head was familiar to any club member of Iron John's gymnasium at the time. Now that he was re-centered and his mind was right, he appreciated the looks, the stares, the whispers. They confirmed that he was a god among men.

Steve Strong focused his mind squarely on a water spot on

the white ceiling tiles as he lay flat on his back and was handed four hundred fifty pounds of solid iron by two gym rats who
were old pals. With every vein in his head, neck, and arms
standing out like knotted roots, Steve snapped the weights out
from his chest and worked them back and forth a half-dozen
times, to the point of utter exhaustion. Steve's face was a fire-
engine red and his equilibrium took a moment of adjustment as
he sat upright on the bench. He opened a bottle of Evian water
and took a long pull.

Out of the corner of his eye he caught a glimpse of someone
who sent cold chills down his back. Mickey Cowden was the
best source in Nashville for any steroid. Didn't matter what you
wanted, how exotic the prescription, how experimental the
product, Cowden could get it. He not only made big pay-offs
to students and teachers at the medical and pharmacy schools,
he was tight with the people at the veterinary schools who
could get the really wild shit. Mickey Cowden, who was only a
middling bodybuilder himself, had become an authority on
drugs and muscle mass. Few medical researchers knew more
about the practical (and impractical) applications of steroid
drugs than Mickey Cowden. Although he had supplied nine-
tenths of the drugs Steve Strong had used, and coached him on
the ways to get the maximum benefit out of them, he had
warned Steve at length that he was way over the line. But still,
he kept on selling them.

Steve made a mental note to give him a wide berth.

"Hear you've been a bit off your mark."

Steve looked up as he zipped up his trousers in the locker
room. It was Mickey Cowden. The weasel actually had the gall
to speak to him.

"Take a hike, fuckwad," Steve answered.

Mickey's mouth dropped open. "*Moi?* Me? Steve, old pal,
what did I do? Was it something I said?"

"Look, ace. I don't need you or the brand of hell you're ped-
dling. Get out of my face and stay out of my face."

"Steve, you seem to forget I was the one who tried to save
your ass. Who else warned you you had gone too far?"

"Everyone. But you're the only asshole who was selling me
the shit."

"Steve, baby, your reality is a little warped. I warned you
repeatedly, *repeatedly*, about your mixing and matching. It had
to catch up with you sooner or later. Too bad we didn't know
about this."

He threw a small vial to Steve Strong, who reflexively caught
it in his massive hand.

"Muscadrol, a brand new direct injectable for racehorses.
Doesn't build a lot of mass, but increases strength like a motherfucker. Safe as candy. This stuff has gotten the cleanest bill of
health of any veterinary pharmaceutical I've ever seen. It's a
wonder drug, man. And get this. When you go off of it, there's
unbelievably high strength retention. You don't lose it. My
sources tell me it will change the face of horse racing forever.
It's so new that I've only turned a few of my closest friends on
to it. Man, they are raving over this shit. And get this—there's
no side effects. No pain, all gain. Not even any mood swings.
No rages, no red face, nothing. Guaranteed to put muscles in
your shit, man."

Steve finished tying his sneakers, snatched up the vial, and
walked up nose-to-nose to Mickey Cowden. He brought his
hand up to Cowden's jaws and with one pincer-like motion
pried open his mouth. He popped the vial in Cowden's mouth
and slapped his chin shut.

"Don't choke on it," Steve said and walked away. He heard
Mickey gagging and spitting and after several minutes of heavy
breathing bolt out of the locker room. Steve smiled at his reflection in the mirror as he combed his golden hair.

As he was leaving the locker room he was stopped cold by a

small box left behind on the locker room bench. Steve's practiced eye knew it contained samples. Pharmaceutical samples. Muscadrol, just as he guessed.

Steve Strong stared at the box a long time. With a grim face and a set jaw he picked up the box, slid it into his shirt pocket, and left without a word to anyone.

Chapter 16

"Where the fuck are we going?"

Carroll and Barry Daniels had spent the morning in training. Both men were exhausted and wringing wet, but Carroll had detoured onto Shelby Drive heading west into the area polite white folks referred to as "the bad part of town." After dark no sane white person would be caught dead driving through South Memphis, a tough, crime-infested sprawl of ghettos, crumbling neighborhoods, and movements in the shadows. Even in broad daylight it took big balls to drive through South Memphis without a case of the sweats.

"It's payback time, and I know who can help me," said Carroll.

"Payback for what?" said Barry.

"That asshole Scud pulled a good fucking practical joke on me. Remember when I told you about that fine broad from New Orleans I was with?"

"Yeah. Sugar Shay, whad'n it? Jeez, what a name."

"She was a setup."

"A setup? By who? Scud?"

"Yeah. He must have sent the bitch up from New Orleans. I will say this, she was one finger-licking good piece of ass. Get this. The next morning I get a package of live crabs delivered to my door from Scud. We ate 'em all at The Bombay, didn't get sick or anything. I woke up a few nights later covered with fucking crab lice."

"Crab lice?"

"Yeah."

Barry roared. They both laughed so hard tears came to their eyes. Carroll's line of vision blurred enough that they almost ran off the road.

"Man, I thought I would scratch my dick off before I found an all-night drugstore open."

They laughed even harder.

"You should have seen the look on the girl's face at the check out counter when she saw me pulling at my crotch and holding onto a bottle of RID. I think she wanted to give me the shit for free."

They bent double in choking fits of laughter, barely able to catch their breaths.

When Barry was breathing normally again he asked, "How could that gal have played it so cool when she was covered up with crotch critters? I can't imagine a woman letting anybody talk her into something like that, even a common street whore."

"I think I've figured it out," said Carroll. "You ever heard of 'rat-fucking'?"

Barry put his hand to his temple and thought for a moment. "Wasn't that in the Woodward and Bernstein book about Watergate? One of Nixon's guys?"

"Yeah. Donald Segretti. It was a term the Watergate bunch used for dirty tricks and off-the-wall guerilla tactics used to fuck-up their political opponents. In the backs of all those *Soldier of Fortune*-type magazines there are all kinds of ads relating to rat-fucking, manuals and products, even classified ads offering expert rat-fucking services. Hell, that's where I stumbled onto the lab where I mail-order cockroaches."

"One of these days you're going to have to 'fess up about those roaches," said Barry. "I'd really like to know why you're raising something people pay good money to get rid of."

"You're not ready for the truth yet, my friend. You couldn't handle it."

"Okay. So what does this have to do with Sugar Shay?"

"The way I figure it, either Scud or Itch stumbled onto those ads. You can buy almost anything from an outfit called EntoLabs out in California, as long as you pass yourself off as a legitimate researcher. They sell chiggers, ticks, a dozen different kinds of mosquitos, you name it. I'll bet Scud bought some crab lice, or more likely, some crab lice larvae or eggs.

"Sugar Shay probably had a little box of the critters in their sterile package waiting in the bathroom all that time. Before we did the wild thang that night, she went in the bathroom and must have mixed up the crab larvae or eggs or whatever into the lubricant she used. Man, that was the slickest sex lubricant I've ever seen. The stuff would not wash off, you could lube an engine with it. I swear I could hardly pee, my dick kept slidin' out of my hand.

"Once she had rubbed that goo all over my pubes, I guess nature took care of the rest. As soon as we were through that night, Sugar asked me in a nice way to leave, said she needed to get her rest. I'll bet you a dollar to a donut she went in the bathroom, washed all that shit off, shampooed her twat with RID about a dozen times, applied a tube or two of ointment, changed into clean clothes, and left the hell for New Orleans. I've got to hand it to Scud, it was a hell of a dirty trick. That's why payback has got to be good."

"Sugar must have owed Scud a big fucking favor," said Barry.

"Yeah, it makes you wonder," said Carroll.

"So what's the game plan?" asked Barry.

"Well, I know for fact Scud was raised around that New Orleans voodoo shit. He takes it seriously. Hell, all those folks in New Orleans do. I want to come up with something that'll scare the shit out of him, and I know who can help me."

"Who?"

"Reverend Hosea down at Voodoo Village."

Barry immediately stopped smiling.

"The fuck you say. I'm not going anywhere near that place."

"Why not?"

"The summer we graduated from Sheffield, a bunch of us got drunk on our asses and somebody dared me to take 'em to Voodoo Village. So about midnight we find the place, drive in, and my front windshield goes 'ka-boom!' and shatters, glass gets all in my hair, down my neck, in my lap, scares the holy shit out of us. Fucking nigs threw a brick through the window. Somebody could have got hurt."

Carroll cleared his throat. "Let me ask you something. You were driving the Roadrunner, right?"

"Yeah."

"And it was loud as shit, right?"

"Yeah."

"And it was after midnight, right?"

"Yeah. What's your point?"

"Reverend Hosea has been bothered by punk white kids since the sixties. They come late at night. Wake everybody up. Throw beer and wine bottles at their windows. Shoot off fire-crackers, and sometimes guns. Scare those folks half to death. Face it, man, we were nothing but a couple of punks ourselves back then."

"I guess so. I'm still not real happy about getting face to face with these nuts. They give me the creeps, if you want to know the truth. But, hey, I'm no party pooper."

"That's more like it, sport. This could be interesting."

❖ ❖ ❖

After driving through miles of urban decay and squalor, they reached the outer edges of Memphis, where houses became sparse and the woods began to deepen. Carroll abruptly slowed and wheeled onto an old gravel access road overgrown with weeds and brush. As the vegetation slapped at the windshield and the gravel rumbled beneath the drivetrain, Carroll and Barry bounced violently several times over deep ruts and holes along the path.

They reached a clearing after another hundred yards. Three small wooden shacks were clustered together and set back from a main house, a ramshackle clapboard affair painted a neon purple. A fat black woman of indeterminate age eyed them suspiciously as she tended what appeared to be a washer and dryer that were crowded together on the tiny front porch. Upon closer inspection, Carroll could tell that the appliances had been ingeniously converted into a barbeque smoker. The woman opened the top of the washer and stabbed at a slab of ribs with a meat fork.

"Wha'chall be wantin'?" the woman scowled at them, wielding the meat fork in a most unwelcome manner.

Carroll and Barry edged closer, Barry having difficulty with his wheelchair on the rough ground.

"Ma'am, we came to seek counsel with Reverend Hosea. He's given me advice and wisdom on spiritual matters before."

"We be needin' a spiritual donation for counsel wit' the Reverend. Twenty dollar."

"Yes ma'am." Carroll handed her a twenty, which she kept wadded in her fist.

"Come on den," the woman beckoned.

They walked around the main house toward the smaller shacks. Carroll and Barry both noticed shades and blinds being pulled tightly and pairs of luminous eyes peering out. As they rounded the back of the main house, Carroll and Barry stopped dead in their tracks. In an open field were displayed dozens of crosses, stars of David, symbols for male and female, large X's, portraits of Martin Luther King Jr. and John F. Kennedy, statuary of St. Francis, St. Christopher, and who knew what else. Much of the bric-a-brac appeared to be homemade.

A low, booming laugh met them from inside the screened-in back porch attached to the main house. Carroll recognized it as belonging to the Reverend Hosea.

"The Lawd giveth and the Lawd taketh away. He done took twenty dollar from you. What you like Him to give *you?*" said the reverend.

"Reverend, a man's done played a powerful trick on my head. He set me up with a beautiful woman, woman whose love was so good she could turn a man to a pillar of salt. But her lovin' visited the devil on me, Reverend, gave me a dose of crabs like to scratch myself to death."

"Some snappin' good pussy, huh?" The reverend laughed long and loud. *Too* long to suit Barry.

"Yes sir. But it was all the devil's trick, a deception. Now I need to show him I've got spirits on my side of the fence. What can you recommend?"

The reverend slowly unlatched the screen door of the back porch and walked towards them. He carried a rosary in one hand and a hand fan in the other. The African robes he wore, combined with his thin, erect frame, gave the reverend an authoritative, magical bearing.

"Hmm. Does this man believe in de world of de spirits?"

"Yes sir. He's from New Orleans and is good friends with some of the reverend mothers."

The reverend squinted his eyes in the hot sun. "They's be powerful conjure womens. But they does so much conjurin' down in New O'lens that de spirits gets mixed up, gets confused sometimes. De spirits out here hears me loud and clear. I'ms the onliest voice."

The reverend spit in the dirt and stirred it with a stick from the yard.

"Tell you whut. Get a plug of the man's hair. Bring it to me and we makes up two charms. One for us to keeps for hexin' and one for him to knows we's hexin' him."

Carroll laughed and said, "Hair, huh? I'll have to figure out how to get it, but believe me, I'll get it. Thanks, Reverend."

"You boys looks a might hongry. You done paid your twenty dollar. Now have some ribs and black-eyed peas wit' us."

"I thought you'd never ask, Reverend. I never smelled anything s'good in my life."

Chapter 17

"**B**uy your own clippers, bitch."

"My, aren't you the good neighbor. Who tinkled in your cornflakes this morning? It sure wasn't me."

Charles and Trist were at it again. The two hairdressers were, at any given moment, the best of friends or the worst of enemies. Their quarreling was a part of the Salon (pronounced with a heavy accent on the first syllable) Plus experience, something that made the fifty-dollar haircuts and hundred-dollar perms seem almost a bargain to the well-heeled patrons. Salon Plus had a wine consultant on retainer, and it was often heard in New Orleans' high places that Salon Plus had a better wine list than most of the city's four-star restaurants.

The scene at Salon Plus, with its ten hairdressers and bevy of hairwashers and manicurists, was a kind of benign chaos, not unlike the backstage madness at an opening night. Charles and Trist were the star attractions and their shouting matches and kiss-and-make-up sessions the source of much gossip in the Crescent City's social swirls.

"Just keep your grubby little hands off my equipment."

"I've seen your equipment, Charles, and it's not enough to get a grubby little hand on."

"You've only seen it when it was off-duty, precious. Check it out when it's on the swing shift."

"Oh, lovely. I'll bring my bifocals."

Scud Matthews sat on a black leather sofa sipping a glass of Bordeaux that was, according to the handout, assertive without being insistent, provocative without being audacious. He was pampered at Salon Plus, and felt that the serious attention his looks were given paid off in terms of the few product endorsements that came his way. His teeth had been straightened and whitened, his scant pockmarks dermabraded into oblivion, and Trist had devised a brush cut that made him look both masculine and chic, no easy feat when the subject was the size and build of a Scud Matthews.

"Scud, sweetheart, how are you babe?" Trist prissed up to Scud and planted a wet kiss on his cheek.

"Getting a little shaggy around the edges," answered Scud. "I need one of your magic makeovers."

Trist rubbed his hand through Scud's hair.

"Oh, my God! You haven't been using that conditioner I gave you have you, you naughty boy? Scud, you're undoing all my hard work here." Trist placed his hands on his hips in exasperation. "Your cut must have a *softness* to it to work. You don't want to look like some sweaty dock worker, do you? My brush cut has to look *hard* and *soft* at the same time."

"Tell me about it," chuckled Charles.

"Excuse me, I was with a customer." Trist fired a comb at Charles that missed by several feet. "Scud, I can't possibly cut your hair if you don't follow my instructions. Raise your hand and repeat after me..."

Scud allowed a smile to play on his lips as he dutifully raised his hand.

"I promise to use a good conditioner," commanded Trist.

"I promise to use a good conditioner," Scud answered mechanically.

"Okay. I'm taking you to Marge. Oh Marge, honey, give Mr. Matthews the full treatment, his texture is just *ruined.*"

Scud endured fifteen minutes of scalding water, glop upon glop agitated into his scalp, and being left with his hair dripping wet. Trist sat him in his styling chair and sprayed a cloud of noxious fumes on his hair. He snipped, trimmed, and clipped for another twenty minutes, blow-dried, brushed, and buffed-out for an extra ten. When Scud looked in the mirror he was reminded why he paid the fifty-plus dollars. "Scavullo, eat your heart out," Scud thought to himself.

Like a yipping lap dog at his heels, Trist kept his nagging on a steady course until Scud was out the door. When Scud was out of earshot Trist shrieked to the heavens, "Why, God, do they bring their damaged hair to *me?*"

As Trist shook Scud's hair from his barber's cape onto the floor, the door exploded open and a large man in dark aviator sunglasses and a plain, dark suit shouted, "Don't touch that hair! You or any of the rest of you!"

The man flashed a shiny badge.

"I'm Agent Fields from the Atlanta Centers for Disease Control. That hair may contain a highly contagious bacterium responsible for a deadly new strain of tuberculosis."

Trist and Charles leapt into each other's arms and Charles began to sob softly.

The man called Agent Fields put on a face mask and rubber gloves and vacuumed every trace of Scud's hair into a portable Red Devil vacuum cleaner. He then carefully placed the vacuum cleaner in a large, thick, clear plastic bag which he sealed completely with masking tape.

He took off his mask, looked into the eyes of the petrified

onlookers, and said, "The Center thanks you for your cooperation. We'll be in touch."

When Trist had calmed down an hour or so later he called Scud and left a message on his answering machine. "Scud, hon, could you please call Trist at your earliest convenience?"

❖ ❖ ❖

The card read, "It's been a hair-raising experience, Ta-ta, Carroll."

Scud knew it was coming and had dreaded the moment. He couldn't imagine why Carroll had gone to all that trouble to collect his hair, but he knew it was something awful.

Scud opened the package with trembling fingers. Inside was a tiny cloth doll with colored beads sewn into it. Pins with black heads on them were jabbed deep into each of the doll's arms. Hair that Scud recognized as his own had been skillfully woven into the doll's head.

"How?" Scud asked himself. "How could Carroll have known about this?"

Scud stood there blankly, holding the voodoo doll for fear of not holding it. He suddenly became light in the head and tiny white meteorites began to blaze in front of his eyeballs. His three-hundred pound frame promptly crumpled to the floor like a sack of raw potatoes.

❖ ❖ ❖

Carroll Thurston hiked twenty minutes into the thickest woods of Shelby Forest, stopped, and unfolded his GI entrenching tool. He dug into a soft patch underneath a swell of leaves and when satisfied he had gone deep enough pulled out a small red flannel bag and tossed it in, covering it carefully with dirt. When the dirt was good and packed, Carroll spread a camouflage of leaves and debris back on top.

The reverend told him the gris-gris bag had to be buried secretly, where no one could find it ever. The bag contained the remainder of Scud's hair and a mixture of herbs and oils that stank to high heaven.

But juju was, after all, juju.

Chapter 18

Carroll had his back to the bar, slicing a lime into bite-sized wedges. When he turned around, a thin veil of light fell in a diagonal across her face. She blew a long, blue plume of smoke out of the downturned corners of her mouth. Her presence had taken him unawares and he didn't immediately know what to say.

"Hi," she said almost sorrowfully, cutting through the strain of silence.

"Jesus, Heather. I didn't expect to see you sitting there. How have you been?"

"So-so. At least I'm alive, I guess." She knocked on the wooden bar for good luck.

"It's been a long time," Carroll said.

"It has," she answered.

"I tried to get in touch with you for at least a couple of months," he said. "I finally gave up."

She didn't answer.

"Can I get you something to drink?" he asked.

"I hear you make a good gin and tonic," she smiled.

"A dignified old black bartender who worked for years at the University Club passed his secret on to me," Carroll said.

He poured a jigger of Tanqueray into a glass with cracked ice in it. He took the hand held spigot he used and filled the glass with tonic. Then he popped a fresh lime wedge into the glass.

"That's it?" Heather asked.

"No. Now comes the tricky part." He took a clean, empty glass and slowly poured the drink into it, ice and all. He set out a cocktail napkin and placed the drink in front of her. "Ta-da!"

"You mean to tell me all you do is pour the drink into an empty glass?"

"Yep."

"That's it?"

"Yep. Taste it."

She brought the drink to her lips and took a small sip. "Not bad. Not bad at all."

"You see," Carroll said, "if you shake things up just a little bit you excite the flavors. Shake it too much and the flavors fall apart. Kind of like relationships. So, are we just going to dance around this thing or are you going to tell me what in hell happened to you?"

"The reason you couldn't reach me all that time is that I was out at Oakville."

"Oakville?"

"Yeah. They had me on a lot of medication. I'm off everything now, thank God, except these damn things." She held up her cigarette.

"My wanting to go out with other women put you in the funny...put you in Oakville? Not to be insensitive, but isn't that kind of drastic?"

"No, Carroll, that's just part of the story. I was carrying a lot of baggage you didn't know about."

"Like what?" Carroll asked.

"Other relationships. Bad ones. Crap you really don't want to hear about."

She lit another cigarette.

"Since when did you start smoking?"

"At Oakville. There was nothing much else to do. I quit for like three years, but with all that happened…"

"They're bad for your health."

"Lots of things are bad for my health, men included. Carroll, I came here tonight to see if we could try again. I'd like to if you would."

"Heather, not a night has gone by that I haven't wondered about you. But I have to be honest, I don't want to be forced to choose between you and anyone else. Don't ask that."

"I won't."

"And, Heather, I don't want to play house either. I like having my own place and living by myself. I like keeping my own schedule."

"I can accept that."

Carroll smiled. "Then maybe you can accept this."

He leaned far over the bar and kissed her like he had wanted to for months. A cluster of lawyers at the opposite end of the bar saw them and cheered, "Hear, hear."

"Want to come over when you get off tonight?" she asked in her sexiest voice.

"Damn, I'm in training."

"You sure?"

"Well, it couldn't hurt just this once, could it?"

"Nah."

Chapter 19

Before Barry Daniels was half out of his van, he was spotted by two children in motorized wheelchairs who threw their controls wide open and raced towards him, crashing into one another deliberately in an effort to be the first to reach him. They held out writing pads covered in shiny, pink patent leather.

"Barry, can we have your autograph, please?" one little girl asked with pleading eyes.

"Sure, honey," he answered.

The air was charged, Carroll Thurston could feel it. As soon as they drove into the tidal basin sized parking lot at Conner Stadium in Dallas for the National Wheelchair Olympics, it was like entering another world, a world in which Barry Daniels ruled a secret kingdom.

By the time they had reached the stadium entrance, a small crowd had begun to gather around Barry. He stopped numerous times to sign autographs for kids—some in wheelchairs, many not—and adults as well. He was hailed by fellow wheelchair athletes nearly every step. Michael Jordan, Nolan Ryan, Mark Spitz, Olga Korbut, celebrated athletes all, had nothing on the hero worship of Barry Daniels this day and this hour in this stadium.

Several television crews were set up to videotape Barry, including a group from ESPN and the BBC. A reporter in a wheelchair from *Sports and Spokes* magazine conducted a lengthy interview.

"Who's this big fellow?" the reporter asked at the conclusion of the interview.

"This is Carroll Thurston, world champion arm wrestler and my training partner," said Barry.

Carroll and the reporter shook hands.

"Gee, you're pretty stout," the reporter said to Carroll. "Too bad you're not a paraplegic. You look like you might be pretty good at this."

He and Barry laughed knowingly. Carroll, however, didn't think the remark was all that damn funny.

Representatives from Windsprint Competition Wear, who had sponsored Barry for the meet, conferred with him at length, asking his opinion on various designs, colors, and accessories while shoving several sets of papers at him to sign. One rep asked to see his racing chair and promptly covered it in corporate decals. They also gave him the latest prototype of their brightly colored aerodynamic clothing, designed to help break down wind resistance.

"At least they're coughing up some money this year," Barry said in an aside to Carroll. "This contract with Windsprint was for five grand. But I get a five grand bonus today if I win and another five grand if I'm lucky enough to break my own world record. They've never dangled that much money before. Pressure, huh?"

"You can do it, man," Carroll said truthfully. "You're stronger, faster, and your technique is improved. Keep the focus. You'll do it."

Barry held up crossed fingers. "Let's hope," he said.

Carroll held up his crossed fingers. "Ditto."

The distance events were finished and the hundred-meter event was announced on the loudspeaker. Barry and Carroll went to the locker rooms, where Barry changed into the Windsprint gear and hoisted himself into his racing chair, which had been meticulously lubed, polished, tightened, and secured. The tire pressure would be gauged numerous times that day to keep the inflation level exact and perfectly balanced. Everything checked.

Barry rolled his racing chair over the track, inspecting the entire hundred meter length for any dips, bumps, or cracks that might throw off his stroke. The track was well-maintained and freshly swept and his eyes spotted no rocks or glass particles that could set him up for disaster, like the flip he had taken several months before on Dwight Road.

He heard his name announced for the first heat. The winner would advance to the final heat, but Barry knew better than take the first heat for granted. His first years in the sport were often filled with frustration and defeat as older, better trained and equipped athletes stomped him right off the starting line. Now Carroll Thurston had added a whole new element to his technique: the power stroke.

Barry's fingers, hands, and wrists were as solid as cold-rolled steel. His grip was unbelievably stronger and he was able to discard the standard padded gloves for thin handball gloves that he covered in rosin. His upper body strength was significantly greater. He owed it all to Carroll Thurston.

Barry rolled to his place on the track with seven other racers and their trainers. Carroll carefully brushed all tiny rock particles and debris from the wheels, which were rechecked a final time for inflation balance. Barry put on his gloves and Carroll quickly gave them a dusting of rosin.

As the starter called "to your marks," Barry took a firm,

measured grip on the top of the push rim and edged forward in
the seat, cocked and ready.

"Set."

"Go!" The starter fired his pistol.

Barry threw down with the force of God and was immediately a length ahead of the pack. His arms pistoned like the fly-
wheels on a raging locomotive and he blazed across the tarmac,
his breathing and downstrokes in a perfect mechanical rhythm.
As he broke through the winner's tape, camera lights flared
from every direction. He bent double, catching his breath,
when it was announced that he had broken his own world
record, 16.12 seconds.

"Five grand!" Barry thought to himself as the stadium
erupted in cheers.

Carroll was beside himself. He jogged out to meet him,
kneeled down, and gave him a bear hug.

"Not so fast," Barry grinned. "Don't forget, I still have the
final heat. Let's not get overconfident."

He squirted water into his mouth from his water bottle,
swished it around, and spit. Barry hopped onto a nearby bench
where he and Carroll examined each tire and tightened down
each spoke. All nuts and bolts were retightened, everything
double-checked. No NASCAR racing engine was more thoroughly tuned than Barry's racing chair.

"Better watch your back, Hot Dog. I'll be breathing down
your neck out there," a competitor told Barry.

It was that smartass from Tallahassee. Bridges something or
other. Barry had to admit it though, Bridges looked good. His
muscles were unbelievably ripped and buffed. He was a Mr.
Universe in a wheelchair.

"If you're breathing down my neck, that means you'll be
behind me. And that's where I intend to keep you," said Barry.
"And while you're back there you can pucker up and kiss my
ass. 'Cause that's all of me you're gonna see."

"Hah. You'll be eating my tire marks, chump."

The final heat was announced over the intercom. Barry was told his lane number and rolled over the course, picking up a couple of pebbles and leaves that had blown onto the track.

Barry and Carroll gave the racing chair one final going over as the starter called out to the racers. The wheels were quickly brushed and Barry's gloves dusted.

"To your marks."

Barry rolled into position. Bridges was two lanes over and tried to give Barry the old evil eye. But Barry was a million miles away.

"Set."

Barry grabbed the rim and leaned forward.

"Go!" The shot rang out.

Whoom!, Barry was down on the push rim with the weight of a bomb, taking the lead instantly. His arms were a blur of motion as he shot toward the finish line. Bridges collided with the racer to his right and they both took hard tumbles. Barry snapped the winner's tape and coasted with his head down a good thirty meters.

The announcement seemed slow in coming, but Barry had broken his own world record again. To Carroll, the stands seemed to empty. Everyone came to congratulate Barry. Camera strobes and flashbulbs created an almost eerie sense of frozen motion as the bodies pulsed. The Windsprint executives did a photo shoot with Barry as they presented him with a check for twenty thousand dollars. They had added an extra five thousand dollar bonus for Barry's second world record.

Even Bridges, with scrapes and bruises all over him, came to congratulate Barry. At the day's closing festivities, Miss Wheelchair U.S.A., a knockout blonde in a wheelchair with a figure to rival Jayne Mansfield's, presented Barry with a medal, ribbons, and a four foot trophy. After she gave Barry the traditional winner's kiss, he whispered in her ear. Her face reddened and she nodded in the affirmative.

"That dog," Carroll laughed to himself.

Barry and Carroll stayed at the stadium well into the night. Barry was pulled in a thousand directions, everyone wanting a piece of him. He signed dozens of autographs, posed for dozens of photos, and still managed to chat with nearly every wheelchair athlete who made it to the playing field. Carroll couldn't help but notice that at least one member of every family that approached Barry was in a wheelchair. "These guys are the *real* sports heroes," Carroll thought to himself.

Barry rolled up with Miss Wheelchair U.S.A. on his arm.

"Carroll old pal, would you mind terribly if some of my friends took you back to the motel tonight? I've made some plans for the evening."

He winked at Carroll. Miss Wheelchair blushed again.

"Sure."

❖ ❖ ❖

Carroll slept like a log at the Motel 8. Barry never made it in. Carroll was ordering the Paul Bunyan Breakfast Special in the motel coffee shop the next morning when Barry finally pulled into the lot. By the time Carroll got back to their room, Barry was lying in his bed, out like a light. Love smells permeated the cramped motel room. Barry didn't wake until six that night. He apologized profusely to Carroll and they decided to leave for Memphis early the next morning.

"Tell you what," said Barry. "Let me treat you to the best bowl of chili in the state of Texas."

"They got Lone Star beer?"

"Hell yeah."

"Let's go, bro'."

❖ ❖ ❖

It was mid-afternoon and the sun hung lazily in the Memphis sky, the Mississippi River a golden sheen in reflection. As always, the Memphis skyline gave its warm welcome, and Carroll and Barry admired it once again in respectful silence. A barge as long as a football field threaded its way beneath the massive pilings of the Mississippi Bridge, the small tug at its side muscling it through the strong current.

Barry exited off the expressway into downtown Memphis.

"Carroll, would you mind me going to my broker's office for a minute before we head home?"

"Not at all. You need to properly invest all that money you just made."

They rode up the elevator of the NBC Building to the offices of Hutchins, Mallory, and Goldstein, where Barry asked to see a Mr. Lewis Hutchins. He told the secretary it was urgent.

Carroll sank into the creamy oxblood leather sofa in the waiting area and thumbed through an old copy of *Architectural Digest* magazine. Barry was shown to the broker's office.

After about ten minutes a secretary approached Carroll.

"Mr. Thurston?"

"Yes?"

"Mr. Daniels and Mr. Hutchins would like to see you for a moment, please."

Carroll cleared his throat. "Well, all right, I guess."

Carroll was shown to a large, handsomely paneled office, obviously a place of wealth and purpose.

"Have a seat, Carroll," Barry said. "I'd like you to meet an old friend of mine, Lewis Hutchins. We've known each other since we were boys."

Lewis Hutchins sat in a motorized wheelchair behind his desk. He smiled and steered his chair around his desk and over to Carroll, then extended his hand. He wore an expensive suit and tie and had fashionable horn-rimmed glasses and a neat, well-clipped beard.

As they shook hands, what had been a faint glimmer of recognition hit Carroll Thurston like a wrecking ball. Through the beard, through the glasses, Carroll knew it was him. There were the beginnings of crow's feet around the eyes and laugh lines around the mouth, but he could clearly see the face of the boy and his tiny body covered in leather and thick metal plates. The eyes cried out to him just as they had twenty-five years before and a thousand dreams later when as a boy Lewis Hutchins was strapped into a battery of braces and allowed to walk at will throughout the Crippled Children's Home. It was rare for Lewis to see able-bodied children at the Home. That's why he had been thrilled to see the Cub Scout wearing such a handsome, colorful uniform. He wanted to touch all the medals and badges. But the Cub Scout was gone before he could reach him.

Carroll held onto Lewis's hand and stared without speaking for a long while. He slowly dropped his chin to his chest and his shoulders began to shake, at first almost imperceptibly, then with greater and greater agitation. He finally broke down completely and wept until God could furnish him no more tears.

Chapter 20

The digital readout tracked higher and higher until Steve Strong at long last hit the magic mark and even nosed a little beyond it. When he was finally through with the robotic arm, the reading glowing back at him was 267.72 pounds of pressure, three-tenths of a pound better than his personal best. Steve Strong laughed like an idiot and slapped the table. Hallelujah, his arm was back! He was in the game.

There was no doubt about it, Muscadrol had saved his career. Mickey Cowden was right: Muscadrol was a miracle drug, no pain, all gain. No 'roid rages, no red face, no nothing. He could practically feel his muscles suck the stuff up. In just three months his arms had become guided missiles, and he was confident that no man in the world could put him down on the mat.

Mickey Cowden had told him that he needed a three or four month grace period for his blood work to come back negative for steroids. Steve had his calendar marked off to the day when the purification would begin. He would load as high as possible until then, his muscles would sing Muscadrol's praises. Cowden had made all the arrangements at the labs for the blood testing to make sure the Muscadrol was completely washed out of his system before the PAWA World Tournament began. Steve didn't want any embarrassing revelations at the tournament. The press would crucify him if any tests came back positive. He could just see the tabloid headlines. The final four months prior to the tournament would consist of a concentrated training regimen, vitamin therapy for blood washing, a special blood-enriching diet, long saunas to sweat out the impurities, and diuretics and purified water to piss out every last ounce of poison.

One of the side perks of Muscadrol was a sense of elation, a permanent feel-good. Steve Strong had never felt so grand, so upbeat and happy, his whole life. Even his knees, as fucked-up as they were, weren't much of a bother.

He had even agreed to go out a second time with a once famous actress who had faded from the limelight. Steve had diplomatically and discreetly pursued her for years, even though she was, according to the gossip columns, happily married. She was still beautiful and still talented, but her reputation as a difficult and erratic performer had, in effect, gotten her blackballed from the back lots of every major studio. The widely publicized comeback of Steve Strong had proven too powerful a lure for an actress in a state of decline, however. She had hinted through intermediaries that she would meet him at a secluded resort in Northern California. Steve flew there, hardly able to believe his good fortune. When she came to her door in the stark altogether, Steve thought he had died and gone to heaven. It was shortly thereafter that Steve learned the actress had a raging cocaine addiction. She complained to Steve that her sinus membranes were eaten alive with septal damage. She then handed him a thin cocktail straw packed with white powder and instructed him to stick it up her ass and blow. She was deathly afraid of needles, she explained, and found it a great way to absorb the cocaine. So Steve did it. It even turned him on a little bit.

Finished with his workout for the day, Steve peeled out of his sweats and turned on the faucets to his two-person home spa, a huge bathtub equipped with Whirlpool jets. Steve decided to celebrate the occasion of breaking his personal best with a handful of Do-Si-Do Girl Scout cookies. He carefully stacked them on the edge of the tub and slipped into the warm, soothing water with an audible, "ahhh." When the water line had crested at his navel, he switched on the Whirlpool jets which began a mild, comforting tempest in the tub. As he settled himself back into the slope of the tub he felt a mild internal jolt that momentarily alarmed him, recalling as it did the seizures that had nearly killed him only a year before. "Just a muscle spasm," he said to himself with relief as he reached for another Do-Si-Do.

The water line was lapping at his chin and he decided to turn off the faucets. He started to lift his arm to pull himself upright in the tub, but to his great surprise his left arm wouldn't budge. He strained and tried again and found that not only would his left arm not move, nothing else—with the exception of his right arm—would move either. He blew the cookie crumbs out of his mouth and began a strangled cry for help. The water had risen to the bottom of his lip, and with his good right arm he desperately began to fend the water away from his mouth. The splashing created waves in the tub which rolled back violently, temporarily submerging his head and sending ropes and sprays of water throughout the bathroom. He struggled to use his right arm to scoot closer to the faucets in the hope he could reach them and shut them off, but his hand could get no purchase on the porcelain and kept sliding out from under him.

Steve Strong began to thrash wildly, causing great swells of water to spill out onto the floor. But the faucets kept pouring and the Whirlpool jets kept whirling. The water level had risen to the top of his lip just below his nostrils when Steve noticed that some of the water had begun to drain off through the overflow holes. But it wasn't draining nearly fast enough.

Splashing the water away finally did no good. It afforded him barely a breath before the water came crashing right back. Mustering the strength remaining in his right arm, he pushed his right side up out of the water and was able to gasp freely for a few short minutes. His arm, however, had begun to tire and was getting heavier and shakier.

"Concentrate!" he ordered himself. He had to find a mental focus, anything, anything at all to center on. With panic seizing him and pain screaming through his arm, he latched onto the image of the beautiful, naked actress and pictured himself once again parting her cheeks, sliding that little straw up her ass, and blowing and blowing and blowing and blowing.

Chapter 21

Carroll leaned forward in the church pew, his head down and his elbows resting on his knees. As the eulogy droned on he nervously drummed his fingers along the spine of a hymn book racked in its pew cradle. "Stupid sonofabitch," is all Carroll could think. "The dumb fuck came this close to biting it once before from shotgunning steroids, and what does he do? He runs right back to them the minute he doesn't perform like Superman."

The Associated Press had called Carroll for a statement. That's how he had found out Steve Strong was dead, dead from drowning in his own bathtub following a stroke. An autopsy revealed freakishly high levels of steroids in his blood. The final report said that the steroids were a major contributing factor to the stroke. After the initial shock wore off, Carroll found himself angry, angry as hell, that Steve Strong had suckered the public and his friends into believing he had kicked. There he was, lecturing school kids on steroid abuse, going on TV and acting like the prince of all recovering addicts, when he was juicing morning, noon, and night. The police had arrested some piece of shit who had been supplying him. Some good that would do now.

The church was filled with people, spectators and reporters, from what Carroll could see. There were only a few arm wrestlers in attendance. Although everyone in the sport admired and respected Steve Strong, he had purposely avoided friendships. Carroll was one of the rare exceptions. Steve was too competitive to view colleagues as anything but the enemy. Somehow Carroll had broken through the barriers. Carroll always believed it was because he never pumped Steve for techniques or tips. Like all the really good pullers, Carroll researched the sport independently. He knew for fact most arm wrestlers gave false or misleading information to throw their opponents off track. Maintaining the edge. That's what they called it. The prevailing wisdom was that only a dumbass would trust the word of another competitor. That's why there were no how-to books on the sport. Even the old-timers guarded their secrets.

The media, to no one's surprise, wore the Steve Strong story out. *Sixty Minutes* repeated its Steve Strong segment with an update on his death. *Hard Copy* and *Current Affair* investigated Steve's personal life, turning up lurid details of his homosexual casting-couch experiences that helped jump-start his career as a celebrity. A once-famous actress laughingly confessed on Howard Stern's radio show that Steve Strong had a peculiar anal fixation and was turned on by administering cocaine rectally with a thin cocktail straw. The radio host immediately sent his staff to get a box of straws and some powdered sugar, and after an hour of coaxing and cajoling talked the actress into an on-the-air reenactment, with blow-by-blow commentary. The ratings shot through the roof and the FCC levied another six-figure fine. The actress soon thereafter was signed to a new multi-picture, multimillion-dollar contract.

The funeral had been a week in coming. The Strawn family was scattered far and wide and had lost touch with Steve.

Lawyers had to sift through the will and estate papers to determine how the funeral expenses would be paid. According to the Nashville newspapers, the remaining family had come after Steve's money like pit bulls off the pit line.

Carroll didn't care about any of that. He just wanted Steve Strong to be remembered as the sport giant he was. But that was the last thing the press seemed interested in. Steve would be remembered as the guy who O.D.ed on steroids and liked to stick straws up ladies' asses. Another chapter for those *Hollywood Babylon* books.

After the third speaker pounded the lectern with his fist warning the assembled of the peril of not accepting Jesus Christ as their Lord and Savior, Carroll had had enough. It was perfectly obvious that not a single one of the speakers had ever met Steve Strong, much less knew him. He nudged Pamela and they both stood up and stalked out during the middle of the sermon.

"They couldn't even give the poor bastard a break during his own funeral," Carroll scowled.

"Even when you die the pitch men keep the commercial running, don't they?" said Pamela.

As they walked out into the sunlight, they were met by twenty microphones and video cameras.

"He's an arm wrestler," one of them yelled as the rest closed in.

"Sir, were you a friend of Steve Strong's?" one asked.

"Yes I was," Carroll answered.

"Any comment on the nature of his death?"

"I wish the media would keep the focus on Steve Strong as an athlete. He owned the sport of arm wrestling for the better part of twenty years and brought it out of the gutter to make it a respectable athletic event. Unless you were locked muscle-to-muscle with Steve Strong, as I was many times, you have no idea of the physical power of the man. There were never over five or six men in the world who could really compete with him. You show me any other athlete in history who can claim a tenure like that."

"Boring," a reporter said loudly, and the group turned *en masse* to pursue someone else.

Byron and Carroll played Whiffleball in the backyard while Pamela prepared dinner. When it was nearing dark Pamela called them in to wash up and laid out a gorgeous table of roast duck with all the trimmings and a nice bottle of chardonnay.

"God, you can cook too!" Carroll laughed and gave Pamela a peck on the cheek and a big hug. Byron, not wanting to miss out, came up and joined in, making it a happy, hugging threesome.

When Byron had gone to bed, Pamela took Carroll by the hand into her bedroom. She locked the bedroom door behind her.

"You don't have anything to worry about this time," Pamela said.

And he didn't.

Chapter 22

B arry Daniels was feeling the burn during his final bench presses in Carroll's weight room when the doorbell rang.

"Goddammit! Who the hell can that be?" Carroll fumed.

"Probably some Jehovah's Witnesses," said Barry. "They were canvassing my neighborhood last week."

Carroll looked out the peephole of his front door and saw two young Asian men in white shirts and ties. On the street he could see a delivery truck. Carroll warily opened the door.

"You Mr. Carroll Thurston?" one of the young men asked.

"Yeah," Carroll answered.

"I'm Michael Wong and this is my brother, John. We're from M.I.T. to set up the machine."

"What machine?"

"No one told you?"

"Told me what?"

"You were left the robotic arm we designed by Mr. Steve Strong. He specified in his will that you get the robotic arm. We brought the arm from Nashville to help you set it up properly. Mr. Steve Strong did not have the robotics set up properly. He only used part of it and his adjustments and calibrations were way off. We checked through his daily records and found his readings off four, five percent. He worked himself half to death."

"I'll be damned."

"We'll bring in the machine and show you how to work it properly. You will get much more benefit than Steve Strong."

Four husky black men sweated and strained bringing in the robotics, which when pieced together were the size of an executive's desk. Barry Daniels immersed himself in the accompanying manual. The two brothers silently and thoroughly engaged all the wires and cables and with the press of one red button fired the grid up.

"You ready to start?" John Wong asked. "You have much to learn. Steve Strong was not so good with our robotics. Michael and I want to make sure you learn it good. It will improve your skills *dramatically*. But you need to pay attention, take good notes."

Carroll excused himself to get several legal pads and pencils. Barry took one of each for himself.

"Let's go," said Carroll.

"I'm right behind you," said Barry.

At the turn of the century, during the golden years of logging, when giant stands of timber were as common a sight as a sky full of migrating geese, lumberjacks had a surefire way of settling old scores. They lined-up three tree stumps in a row and sank double-bladed axes into the two at opposite ends. The axes were sharpened to an edge so fine they could be used to shave. The lumber-jacks would use the middle stump to arm wrestle, the loser watching in horror as the exposed blade on the end stump buried itself shank deep in flesh and gristle.

In the ages that came before, pitting arm against arm, strength against strength, was one of man's most popular forms of sport and duel. In the orient they used sharp-ened bamboo as their touch pad targets, in India cobras, in the American West live scorpions. Modern times, of course, permit no such cruelty, thus the strongest and ablest strive to become bigger and stronger and faster, until with muscle power alone they can rend bone from marrow. There is no longer a need for axes, knives, or poisonous snakes. Man against man is enough.

Chapter 23

When the bellboy approached Carroll Thurston, Carroll insisted on carrying one small travelling case himself. The big hotel sign outside, in four-foot dancing lights, welcomed all the arm wrestlers with the message, The PAWA and the Glory. Welcome PAWA World Tournament.

Carroll paused a moment to take in the grandeur of the lobby of the Kensington Hotel of St. Louis, which was a match even for the ornate lobby of the Peabody in Memphis. He spotted at least a dozen familiar faces, one or two of whom were super heavyweights, like himself. There were even more faces he didn't recognize, but he could tell from their hypertrophic forearms and the curious way they carried them that they had to be arm wrestlers.

As Carroll checked in at the front desk, an old man in a polyester suit the color of key lime pie tapped him on the shoulder. His wife, who had just a touch of blueing in her grey perm, smiled meekly at his side.

"Say, what are you fellas part of anyway?" the old man asked.

"We're arm wrestlers. We're competing in a world tournament here," said Carroll.

"Oh, I see. Some of that action like on TV." He rocked his arm back and forth in imitation of the arm wrestlers he had seen.

"Yes sir." Carroll turned his attention back to the front desk. The old man tapped his shoulder again.

"Say, you ever hear of Roy Thomas, over to Des Moines?"

"No sir, never have."

"Well, you should have. Strongest boy I ever saw. You oughtta see what that fella can do with a bale of hay. I'll just bet you he'd give you a heck of a run for your money." The old man guffawed, pleased with his bluster.

Carroll wheeled on the old man and put his face within an inch of the old man's.

"Do you know what I'd do to your hay baler, old man? You ever see what a corn picker can do to a man's hand? That's nothing compared to what I'd do. I'd rip his arm off at the root and eat it with ketchup and onions right in front of him. Then I'd pick my teeth with his bones. What do you say to that?"

"Well, uh, I..."

Carroll zipped open his jacket and pointed to the wording on his T-shirt.

"We're MEAT EATERS, KILLERS, and SUCKERS OF BLOOD. Amateurs and hay balers wipe our butts and fetch our beers."

The old man grabbed his wife, who was shaking like a leaf, and hustled her out of the lobby. Carroll could see the old man fumble for a prescription bottle and put a tiny white pill under his tongue.

"Hey, that was a good 'un, Carroll," a mountain of a man said as he slapped Carroll on the back. Carroll could hear other arm wrestlers laughing too. Which was good, since he had scared the old man more or less for their benefit. Carroll had the taste of blood in his mouth, and it tasted good.

"Snack Pack Harris!" Carroll said to the four hundred-plus-pound man. "You been on a diet?"

"Shoot naw," answered Snack Pack in the same high spirit he always did. Good insults were wasted on the man. "Hell, if anything I've picked up a few pounds. Momma's biscuits and gravy'll do that to you. Say, you were a friend of Steve Strong's, weren't you?" Snack Pack continued.

"Yeah, I was."

"Too bad about him," Snack Pack said sincerely. "Never saw the use of that steroid stuff myself. Hell, I got all the muscle I need. Speed's always been my downfall. You skinny three hundred pound boys just seem to get around faster. Say, you hear about Scud Matthews?"

All kinds of weird rumors had been floating around about Scud.

"I've heard a few things," said Carroll. "What about you?"

"They say the ole boy's been sick as a yellow dog. Folks been sayin' he's got AIDS or something. Been in the hospital a few times is what I heard. I guess he caught something from queerin' around and all. Wonder if he'll make it to the tournament?"

"Tom King said Itch signed Scud up two months ago on the first day of registration," said Carroll. "Nobody's heard from him since."

Several people had told Carroll through the wrestling grapevine that somebody had hoodooed Scud bad, that everything in his life had turned to thin shit. He supposedly was food-poisoned, lost his job at the porno shop, was evicted from his apartment in the French Quarter, got a dose of the clap, and now there were persistent rumors about AIDS. One thing was sure. Scud had gone into hiding. None of Carroll's New Orleans spies had seen hide nor hank of the man. No one knew where he had been training or even *if* he had been training. One rumor had it that Scud had been whacked by the Mafia. It was all very strange, but everything Scud ever did was borderline goofy anyway.

With or without Scud, Carroll knew he had his work cut out for him at the tournament. Snack Pack Harris was a trailer load of hurt all by himself. Even with Steve Strong no longer part of the picture and Scud looking iffy, there were over forty competitors in the super heavyweight class. Over three hundred arm wrestlers had registered for the tournament coming from every corner of the globe. In the lighter weight categories, the Middle East was exceptionally strong, as well as India, Japan, and the Phillipines. The heavyweight classes were dominated by Americans and Canadians, but the Swedes, Irish, and Russians had been making serious inroads. However, the ban on steroids gave the PAWA World Tournament a clean slate, a level playing field. Carroll knew that there were a lot of pullers who wouldn't be squat without them. For example, everyone knew how good Scud Matthews was with the juice. The question was, how good would he be without it?

At least the money was right. ESPN was covering the event and Goldcrest Beer had ponied up twenty thousand dollars for each winner, with the exception of the super heavyweight class, which had an upfront guarantee of thirty thousand. As in boxing, the heavier weight classifications drew more interest and attention, therefore more money. Word had it that several product endorsements had come through, which could make for ten or fifteen grand more. Not bad for a single day's take. If you were the winner.

Carroll had hurt both Heather and Barry Daniels's feelings when he refused to take them along with him to St. Louis. He had tried to explain that he had to be totally psyched and centered and they would be distractions. But there was more to it than that. Carroll almost literally became another person the minute he stepped up to the Jeffrey table. He wasn't even sure at that point he was human anymore. At that table total war would be declared and it was, as one reporter put it, "a cold, heartless combat." Every nuke at his disposal, he would use. He would scorch the earth and salt the ground. Arm wrestlers were the most intense mindfuckers of any competitive sport. If you weren't *of* it, you wouldn't understand.

At 10:00 p.m. Carroll Thurston stepped into the bar of the Kensington Hotel like the bad guy in a wild West showdown. He stood silently in the middle of the room, making sure every puller got a good look at him and the inscription—MEAT EATER, KILLER, & SUCKER OF BLOOD—on his T-shirt.

He grabbed the arm of a passing waitress and told her to bring him two Killian's and two glasses of water in *exactly* thirty minutes.

He arranged two chairs on either side of him and dramatically swung them into a "Y" position over his head as all conversation in the bar ceased. He began stoking the fires of hate with images of his old boss, Bernie Kelso. Kelso showering him with specks of spit as his putrid breath warmed his face, Kelso scanning a roomful of executives like a movie Terminator, talleying infractions, his gold shark-figure cuff links glinting under the cold luminescence of a fluorescent light.

The chairs held steady as Kelso spewed invective, but as the image fixed itself squarely in Carroll's mind, Kelso's visage suddenly melted into the smiling face of Byron's. Carroll shook his head and the chairs dipped deeply, eliciting catcalls from the dozens of pullers packed into the bar. He had locked into the image of Kelso again when without warning the face dissipated into nothingness.

The chairs touched the floor. Carroll was drained and drenched in perspiration. The waitress was nowhere to be found.

Carroll checked his watch. Only ten minutes had elapsed.

He turned a chair over and immediately understood. Lead weights had been superglued to the bottom. He went to another table and turned over a chair. Lead weights. And another. And another.

The whole room was convulsed in laughter. Carroll smirked, wiped his brow, and slung sweat out at the crowd.

Hell, he'd been had. He figured he may as well be a good sport about it.

Out of the corner of his eye Carroll noticed Itch sitting off by himself at the bar, grinning a toothy grin from ear to ear.

"Itch, Itch, Itch," Carroll said out loud as it dawned on him who was responsible. "I never knew you had teeth."

"Touché, motherfucker," Itch said as he smiled even more broadly and held out a beer glass in toast.

Chapter 24

Carroll Thurston was as ready as he would ever be. He had trained with a zealot's fervor for the better part of a year. He had pulled at least once a week with the best training partner he ever had, Barry Daniels. Weight training, running, rope climbing, hanging, and reflex exercises could take you as far as you needed to go conditioning-wise. But the elements of surprise and human variation could come only from pulling.

The small band of amateur pullers in Memphis was totally outgunned by Carroll's arm power. Carroll found it necessary to travel out of town once or twice a month to have a go at capable, competitive pullers. He and Steve Strong at one time had met frequently to pull. Snack Pack Harris was always worth the trip to Alabama for pulls. Snack Pack had greater holding power than anyone in the sport. With his weight behind him, he was unbeatable. Carroll had learned a lot by purposely placing himself in a losing position and fighting creatively against the tide of Snack Pack Harris.

Barry Daniels could have been, as the saying went, a contender. But Barry had other fish to fry in a sport for which he

was custom-tailored. As a puller, he was no match for Carroll
Thurston, it was true. He was lightning quick, however, and
could put a dozen smart moves on Carroll, always keeping him
on his toes, always keeping him guessing.

The robotic arm had been a godsend. Barry was a whiz at
programming its computer, and together they filled the disk
drive with stats from the top pullers. By reviewing hours of
tournament videotapes, they programmed in likely moves,
weaknesses, and strengths and were able to stage mock pulls
with the computer's analysis of the best countermoves. The
robotics had allowed Carroll test pulls with Scud Matthews,
Snack Pack Harris, Buddy Solomon, Ingmar Axberg, Ashok
Jallepalli, and even the late Steve Strong.

Carroll held up his forearm in the mirror and flexed it, causing the muscles to fan out like a cobra spreading its hood. He
smiled confidently and zipped into his warm-up jacket. He
picked up his small travelling case and left to catch the elevator.

The super heavyweights weren't scheduled until 4:00 p.m.
as the day's final event, but Carroll went to the one o'clock
opening ceremony anyway, partly because he liked to study
the lighter weight pullers. They unfailingly put on the best
show and had the quickest moves, but Carroll mainly went
because he wanted to be seen and make his presence *felt*. The
cavernous ballroom of the Kensington Hotel was filled with
risers surrounding a tournament stage and banks of television
lights that blanketed the arena in high-wattage illumination.

He was tagged by a television crew as soon as he walked in.

"Standing beside me is one of the all-time great super heavy-
weights, Carroll Thurston from Memphis. Carroll, in the last
PAWA Tournament you placed second, going down in defeat to
Scud Matthews. Anything you'll be doing different this time out?"

"Well, I doubt that I'll be pulling with Scud."

"And why is that, Carroll?"

"Simple. He won't be pumped-up on steroids this time due to the new rules for disqualification. Without 'em he's nothing but a tulip-sniffing candyass. He'll blow out after two pulls."

"There are rumors that Matthews has been battling serious illness. Have you heard anything to confirm this?"

"He'll be here all right. Bet on it. No way he'll pass up an opportunity to win thirty-five grand."

"And there you have it from Carroll Thurston. Now a word from our sponsor."

The lightweight pullers had gone at each other like starving yard dogs all afternoon, the television cameras capturing every second of strain and pain in super close-up. The action had been thermonuclear and a lot of the juice jockeys of past tournaments had gone down in flames and wreckage.

"How sweet it is!" middleweight champ Bob McGrath had yelled when he pulverized his long-time nemesis, Ace Carrington, who had been a vocal proponent of steroids for years. The mood had definitely changed.

Carroll had watched silently from a shadowed area of the risers until the weigh-in was called for the super heavyweights. Snack Pack Harris weighed in at 427 pounds and the tournament officials had to recalibrate the scales when he got off. Carroll came in at 304 and was reaching to pick up his bag when he saw Itch and Scud walk in. A hush fell over the group as Scud shuffled to the scales. He looked as if he had been dead ten years. Hard, dark circles ringed his eyes and the pallor of his skin was fish-belly white. His beard was unruly and unkempt, his hair matted in the back as if he had slept in bed for weeks. A cheesy, unwashed musk wafted through the room, twining the nose hairs of each puller.

"Two eighty-seven," the official announced as he checked the scales.

"He hasn't lost much weight to look that sick," Carroll thought to himself.

As the double elimination match got underway, Carroll unzipped his warm-up jacket revealing his MEAT EATER, KILLER, & SUCKER OF BLOOD T-shirt. He slid a dancer's leg warmer onto his right arm to keep the muscles warm, and began light pulling with a rolled-up beach towel to loosen and lubricate the joints and ligaments and put some elasticity in the muscle groups.

Scud stood feebly as Itch unbuttoned his athletic jacket. He and Itch wore matching T-shirts that read SUPPORT AIDS AWARENESS. As soon as he was out of his jacket, Scud sat down and rested his head and folded arms on his knees.

Snack Pack Harris didn't do a thing.

Chapter 25

"M atthews and Grady on deck," came the announcement
from the arena.

The entire group of super heavyweights walked through the
aisle between risers to the staging area to an eruption of cheers
and hollers. Itch helped Scud wearily climb the steps to the
stage and walked him to the rosin bowl where he coated Scud's
hands liberally in rosin. Mike "Slowhand" Grady did the same.

As the two pullers went to their respective places at the
Jeffrey table, Mike Grady squinted hard at an open, bloody
sore on the back of Scud's right hand that had soaked through
the rosin.

"Hey, ref," Grady shouted over the crowd chatter. "You
don't expect me to pull with that thing on his hand, do you?"

The ref examined the hand and called over the physician on
duty. The doctor looked the wound over and said to Scud,
"Anything you want to tell us about this, son?"

"It's a sore. What else is there to say?" Scud answered, seemingly exhausted.

The ref and doctor conferred for a moment and the ref said,

"Scud, you have to put a bandage on that. We can't have wrestlers with open sores bleeding all over everybody."

"Fine with me," said Scud dryly.

The physician peeled off a big square Band-Aid and stuck it to the back of Scud's hand.

"Allright gentlemen," the ref said.

"Hold it," Grady said sternly. "I refuse to pull with some fag asshole who's got AIDS."

"What AIDS?" Scud asked without a trace of humor.

"Listen, Grady," said the ref. "We have no way of knowing if Matthews has a damn thing. His sore is covered up. So either step up or forfeit."

"I forfeit. Under protest."

"That's it, then," said the ref. "Thurston and Rawlins, next on deck."

Carroll peeled off the leg warmer on his arm and picked up his travelling case. He stepped up to the Jeffrey table for a moment and asked the ref for a table wipe-down. He set the travel case by the left leg of the table and walked to the rosin bowl.

Luke Rawlins stormed to the stage, wild-eyed and stripped to the waist. He wore baggy cotton shorts that tightened around the waist with a draw-string. He was barefoot as well. Rawlins' torso was a Sistine Chapel of ugly tattoos, human skulls being the recurrent motif. He plunged his hands into the rosin and howled.

"You ugly meatbag muthafucka, piece of shit, scum-sucking..." Rawlins hurled the words as loud and fast as his big mouth could get them out and pounded the table to add effect.

As he leaned in towards Carroll's face, Carroll said, "Pardon me, Luke," and casually reached down to re-tie his shoelaces.

Thrown off-pace momentarily, Luke Rawlins reached into the brown grocery sack he had brought with him and took out a quart of Quaker State Motor Oil and an old church key-type can opener.

"Steve Strong's old trick," Carroll said to himself.

Rawlins laughed like a madman, opened the can, and quaffed the entire quart.

He looked Carroll square in the eye triumphantly and belched a loud bubble of sour gas. Rawlins put his elbow into the table cup and wrapped his fingers tightly around the hand peg when he was seized with a shudder and felt a rolling wave bolt from his stomach. His mouth opened and Quaker State Motor Oil shot with great force past Carroll Thurston's right shoulder onto several rows of screaming spectators. Rawlins fell to his knees, heaving great puddles of greenish fluid onto the stage.

"Forfeit!" called the ref. "And a clean-up."

Snack Pack Harris was called to the table next, pitted against a newcomer with quiet menace and a reputation for fireball takedowns. Andy McLarty glared across the table line at Snack Pack, who smiled back good-naturedly.

"Get a grip," said the ref.

The pullers worked their palms and fingers in together and as they began to feel each other's strengths, the grip broke.

"Again," said the ref.

They curled their fingers back together and began to test one another with mild loading.

"Careful with the loading," warned the ref.

They backed the pressure off slightly.

"Ready?"

The ref placed his hands on top of the grip.

"Ready," said McLarty.

"Ready," said Snack Pack Harris.

"Go!"

Snack Pack Harris moved his shoulder into the middle of the table as soon as he heard the "guh" sound of the word go, blocking McLarty from a quick offensive takedown. Harris began to squat in place, using his full four hundred-plus pound weight to drag down the opponent to the touch pad. McLarty's forearm was caught in an awkward position that no experienced puller would have fought against. He was young and ambitious enough to think there was a chance of recovery. He was wrong.

As McLarty exerted every ounce of muscle he had, there was a loud pop, like the high-pitched report of a .22 caliber rifle, and Andy McLarty's face became a picture of pain. He hit the pad with a loud "whoomp."

Snack Pack Harris looked directly into the closest television camera, shrugged his shoulders, and said, "Damn, I broke another one."

Scud Matthews was called up next, going head-to-head with Buddy Solomon of Israel, a no-nonsense pro. Scud was barely able to make it to the wrestling table and was wheezing and visibly out of breath. He stared vacantly into space as the referee set them up and gave the go. His reaction was a fraction late and Buddy Solomon easily forced him off balance and slammed him with authority to the mat. Scud would be blown out of the running with one more loss.

Later in the tournament Scud easily overpowered a clumsy, overmatched rookie named Wayne Echols, but looked so bad doing it Carroll was beginning to wonder if the AIDS rumors might be true. Two other pullers forfeited by refusing to touch Scud's bandaged hand, which edged him up higher in the day's rankings.

Ingmar Axberg of Sweden, nicknamed "The Flash" for his speed, had Snack Pack Harris pinned before anyone had blinked. The television announcers had to replay the action in slow motion several times to see exactly what happened.

The field had narrowed sharply. Of the 43 entrants, only seven hadn't crapped out. The rookies had pretty much cancelled one another, leaving the field open, as always, to the old pros.

"Harris and Thurston, on deck."

Carroll always dreaded his one-on-ones with Snack Pack Harris. If the least thing went wrong, it was all over. You simply could not recover from a bungled move with Snack Pack Harris.

As they worked into the grip, Carroll wrapped his right leg around the table leg for extra support and felt Harris digging into the tender spot at his thumb base. But Carroll was prepared for that and flexed his hand muscles to let Harris know it didn't mean shit.

"Ready?"

"Ready."

"Ready."

"Go!"

Carroll tried to cut inside, but Harris forced his own wrist downward in a counterclockwise rotation, attacking Carroll's hand balance and strength. Once Snack Pack Harris had gained the dominant position, it was simply a matter of dragging Carroll down.

"Well, Carroll," Snack Pack said jovially when they left the stage, "it's like my Momma always said. If at first you don't succeed, keep on suckin' 'til you do seed."

As in the last PAWA tournament, this one came down to three finalists: Carroll Thurston, Scud Matthews, and Snack Pack Harris. No one at the tournament was the least bit surprised, even if Scud looked like Keith Richards with forty extra miles of bad road and had advanced largely through the forfeits of the others.

The Flash had taken out Buddy Solomon and Ashok Jallepalli. Mike "Slowhand" Grady had managed to stop The Flash, but was himself wiped off the board when he refused for the second time to pull against Scud Matthews. The Flash was taken out of the competition when Carroll Thurston threw a surprise blocking maneuver on him, one which he had rehearsed endlessly with his robotics. As the referee began the count-off, Carroll, rather than gripping the hand-peg as usual, pushed against it with the palm of his hand, forcing his massive shoulder instantly to the far right of his side of the table. The move, a risky one, effectively prevented another one of The Flash's booming takedowns, turning the match instead into an issue of power. Carroll quickly snapped his wrist counterclockwise, further weakening The Flash's already precarious position, and slowly bowed him to the touch pad.

"Harris and Matthews, on deck."

Scud was again led to the stage by Itch and shuffled over to the table after rosin dusting.

"Well, if it isn't Jabba the Gut," said Scud with a flicker of his old sarcasm.

"Well, if it ain't the return of the living fucking dead," answered Snack Pack.

At the go, Scud, using surprising speed and a variety of rapid-fire twisting wrist maneuvers, whipped Harris' arm to the touch pad for the pin.

"There goes my new John Deere," Snack Pack wailed to the TV announcers.

Carroll and Scud shot looks at one another and smiled. Déjà vu all over again.

Chapter 26

After a brief rest, the announcement came over the loud-speakers, "Thurston and Matthews, on deck." The crowd was baited and ready.

Itch led Scud to the stage and they waited silently at the rosin bowl to dust up.

Scud and Carroll approached the Jeffrey table at the same time and Scud put his elbow in the cup and worked his arm into it until it felt right. Carroll reached into his small travel case and removed a large Thermos bottle.

"Need a shot of Gatorade, old man?" Scud sneered.

"Yeah, just a little picker-upper," said Carroll.

He unscrewed the cap and cockroaches swarmed out of the opening. Carroll grabbed a handful and chewed them with a wide open mouth. He emptied more into his hand and flicked them at Scud, who jumped like a kangaroo. Carroll slung several fistfuls at shrieking spectators and the camera crews. The TV picture showed a videocam dropping to a stage floor alive with feet and cockroaches.

One of the security guards on duty panicked and began blasting away at the roaches with his service revolver. When things had finally calmed down, half the audience had fled for the exits and the stage platform was perforated with gaping holes.

"Warning," said the ref after taking several minutes to regain his composure. "Man, don't ever do that again," he added for effect.

"You bastard," said Scud. "I wish I had thought of that."

"Get a grip," said the ref, still in shock.

As they mounted up at the table, Scud drew his lips from his teeth and said while reading Carroll's T-shirt, "So, you're a MEAT EATER, KILLER, & SUCKER OF BLOOD? Why don't you suck this?"

Scud turned his ring backwards and slapped it across the open palm of his right hand, causing a tiny spurt of blood. The ring had sharp, raised edges of a type common among prison inmates who use them as a weapon.

Carroll instantly grabbed Scud's hand and bent down to lick the blood.

Scud jerked his hand back as if it had been scalded.

Carroll rolled the tip of his tongue around the edges of his teeth, blood still visible against the enamel.

"Warning!" cried the ref. "Doctor, wipe that blood off and let's fix him up with another bandage."

"AIDS my ass," Carroll laughed in Scud's face.

"Well folks, we've seen it *all* at the PAWA Tournament today," the weary TV announcer said into the camera.

"Okay boys, get those elbows down, and no more foolishness," said the referee after Scud was cleaned up.

They carefully wrapped their wrists together and locked eyes.

"Ready?"

"Ready."

"Ready."

"Go!" The ref immediately removed his hands.

Their grip instantly broke apart.

"Okay boys. Mount up again. And watch the loading."

They slowly worked their hands together into another knot of muscle and sinew.

"Ready?"

"Ready."

"Ready."

"Go!"

The grip broke again.

"Okay fellas. One more time."

They silently fell back into place. The referee said the magic word and Scud's elbow slipped out of the table cup.

The crowd began to jeer.

"I've got all fucking day, Scud," Carroll smiled.

"Well, gentlemen, I haven't got all day," the annoyed ref barked at them. "If it happens again I'll be forced to strap you together or disqualify the one of you who's pissed me off the worst. Have I made myself clear?" He eyed Scud.

"Clear as a sunny day," Scud grinned.

"Ready then?"

"Ready."

"Ready."

"Go!"

When the adrenaline began to surge Carroll was always surprised at how the world seemed to turn into a slow motion water ballet, the sounds and cries of everything around him sucked into a noiseless vacuum. He looked across the table line at Scud, saw his eyes focused in deep concentration on the touch pad, on the spot where he intended to force Carroll's hand. As Carroll felt his arm shoot forward, he watched Scud's eyes, knowing they would narrow when he began one of his wrist moves. Like the great baseball player Ty Cobb, Carroll Thurston considered himself a "scientific" athlete, a man who carefully studied the sport and exploited his competitor's every weakness. He watched the eyes, the facial mannerisms, nervous habits, breathing, all the little clues that telegraphed a puller's intentions.

Scud, moving with the sharpened reflexes of a jungle animal, fired his wrist downward...snaking, twisting, a writhing rope of coiled muscle.

"Let him, let him..." Carroll whispered to himself.

Scud fought hard to bring his wrist over the top to gain the dominant position. In the disturbing quiet of the moment Carroll felt Scud's push and his power and saw his eyes alight when he felt the first flush of the win.

"Now!" Carroll shouted to himself as he crashed the heel of his hand with piledriving force into the thick of Scud's forearm.

"Surprise, motherfucker," were the words that hummed in the back of his brain as he hammered down with full strength. He laughed to himself as he saw the alarm in Scud's eyes. Always the eyes, he thought.

As Scud's arm arced backwards, he tried to recover by pulling Carroll's arm towards his chest. There was one moment, a slip of time, when the two pullers seemed to freeze in place. The spectators and sports announcers held their breaths.

Scud jerked his arm once, and jerked it again without changing their position in the slightest. As Carroll leaned into his move, the heel of his hand drove harder into Scud's forearm, weakening his remaining leverage.

All color and sound seemed to drain from Carroll's senses as Scud's arm crept snail-like towards the touch pad. It seemed as if Scud must have had time for a hundred countermoves, but Carroll knew in real time it had to be all over. Carroll could make out a muffled yell as he watched, as if he had a silent inner spectator, Scud's arm bow backwards and gently kiss the touch pad.

Wham! The sound of Scud's hand slapping the touch pad leather with a loud fury echoed in Carroll's ears. Within a split second, sights and sounds from every conceivable direction roared to his senses, like an alarm clock pulling him out of a heavy sleep.

Cheers from the audience drowned out the official announcement that Carroll Thurston was the world's new super heavyweight arm wrestling champion. Carroll and Scud would both be required to submit urine specimens for steroid analysis, but pending the results, Carroll Thurston was the new big dog.

Carroll lifted his arms high above his head in a sign of victory, his skin slick and gleaming with sweat under the bright television lights. The crowd was on its feet, the roar of approval nearly deafening. A small girl came forward with a bundle of roses, which Carroll gracefully accepted and waved for the audience to see.

Carroll turned toward Scud Matthews as a sportsmanlike gesture and began to applaud him, and the audience followed in kind. But Scud hadn't moved from the table. He appeared to be dazed and disoriented. Itch quickly made his way to him through the crowd. Suddenly Scud slumped to the floor as the audience collectively gasped. His body began to jerk spasmodically and his eyes rolled up into his head.

Itch began to wail uncontrollably, sobbing for someone to get the tournament doctor who rushed out of the locker room, where he had been treating Luke Rawlins for nausea and vomiting. The doctor turned on a tiny light and looked into Scud's eyes. He then felt his pulse.

"I can't tell a thing here. We'd better get him to a hospital," the doctor said.

A stretcher was brought and four arm wrestlers volunteered to help Scud to an ambulance. As Scud was carried past Carroll, Carroll noticed one eyelid flutter and wink at him. There was no mistaking it. Scud's body then jerked in another series of violent spasms.

"And to think I almost felt sorry for that sonofabitch," Carroll thought to himself.

As Carroll shook his head in disgust and began to towel off, a microphone was thrust in his face and a camera crew surrounded him.

"Congratulations, Carroll Thurston, the new winner of the PAWA super heavyweight title. How does it feel, champ?"

"A hell of a lot better than it did four years ago."

"What does it take, Carroll, to make it to the top of the arm wrestling profession?"

Carroll paused. "You ever seen a three-legged man at a county fair?"

"Can't say I have, Carroll."

"The champions you see here today have a lot more in common with a three-legged man than the guy at home watching this on TV. See, we're all freaks. Freaks of nature. We come out of the womb ten times stronger than an average man. That's why bar matches are so unfair. The men you see here at the PAWA Tournament, the consistent winners, are a quantum leap from small-town tough guys. Throw in training techniques and the freaks become even freakier. Ever seen Ted Williams or Mickey Mantle hit a ball?"

"Sure."

"Not one in a billion people can hit a tiny white object whistling at them at a hundred miles an hour with a big stick like that. Those guys are statistically more abnormal than men with three legs. You just aren't aware of that abnormality until they're standing there at home plate with a bat in their hands. A man who can break another man's arm like spun glass with nothing more than muscle and bone is a freak. I can't think of any other word to describe it."

With that, Carroll turned and walked out of camera range.

Chapter 27

Carroll didn't think he had the energy to shake one more hand. He was tired to the bone, the kind of tired that can only come from a year's sweat and blood directed towards one goal. And he held that goal in his hands, all twenty pounds of it, a trophy that stood waist-high and a foot deep. He touched his pants pocket and felt the bulge, a bulge comprised of one PAWA tournament check and six checks from corporate sponsors. For the first time in his life he had a measure of economic freedom, but he was far too exhausted to give it more than a passing thought. All he could think of was taking his phone off the hook, hanging the DO NOT DISTURB sign outside his door, and burying his face in a soft pillow. He knew he would be sore as hell for several days, but fifty thousand dollars would buy a lot of rubbing alcohol.

As he walked down the hallway of the hotel, fumbling in his pocket for his room key, he noticed rose petals scattered on the floor. It wasn't until he got to his room number that he noticed the trail led to his door. A red ribbon was tied fancily around the doorknob. Puzzled, he opened the door and stopped in his tracks. Heather was lying on his bed atop a layer of the rose petals, a long-stemmed rose clamped between her teeth. She wasn't wearing a stitch.

Heather purred like a cat.

"Heather, wow, I don't know what to say," Carroll said as he felt the familiar stirrings below his waist.

"Don't say anything, big boy. Just come and give me some of that champeen lovin'." She purred again.

Carroll obediently dropped his trophy and walked to her as she stood up on the bed. He buried his face between her soft breasts and cupped a meaty buttock in each hand, kneading them as if they were dough. Heather sighed with pleasure.

She reached down and unbuttoned his polo shirt and pulled it over his head. She twirled it like a lasso and let it go to fly across the room. Carroll watched as she nimbly worked at his belt and the fastenings on his trousers. Within moments he was fully naked and fully erect. Heather laid back on the bed and patted the spot next to her.

As Heather's thighs parted and Carroll positioned himself, he collapsed on top of her. His weight forced most of the air out of her lungs.

"Carroll...Carroll honey, I can't breathe."

"I'm sorry, but I just can't do it," he said as he rolled off her and hung his head in shame.

"Don't worry, sweetheart. These things happen to all men sooner or later. Let's give it a few minutes. It'll pass."

"No, it's not that. I just can't do it."

Heather blinked. "I don't understand, honey. What do you mean?"

"I don't know. It just doesn't feel right. I'm sitting here and one part of me wants you so bad I could cry. But there's another part of me that for once in my life is saying no."

"Does this have anything to do with that woman with the boy in Nashville?"

"I'm afraid so. I'm really sorry, Heather."

"Dammit, Carroll, I thought we had worked out an agreement about her. I guess now that you're a world champion, I'm not good enough for you anymore."

"Heather, you've got to stop it with that kind of self-pitying crap. I'm not going to sit here and let you go to pieces just because I've had a change of heart. Haven't you heard, Heather, *shit happens*, and shit happens to everybody, not just you."

"One, two, three, four..."

"What are you doing?"

"Counting to ten so I don't break a lamp over your fucking head...five, six, seven, eight, nine, ten." She took in a deep breath. "Okay, Carroll. Why the big change? Why the change right when we're naked and drooling?"

"I honestly don't know. It just hit me all at once. It just seemed wrong to go through with it. I'm crazy about you and that's the God's honest truth. I think you're beautiful, I love your company, you're fun just to be with and talk to. And you're a hellcat in bed. No doubts on that score. But with Pamela and Byron, it's like I *belong* there. It's like they need me, like we answer something in each other."

"Is it that you're just finally really in love, Carroll, and are too stupid to recognize it?" Heather snapped.

"I've always heard that love was just a state of temporary insanity. With them it's different. It's like we fit, like we're all pieces of a jigsaw puzzle that fit together perfectly."

"Maybe love's not insanity at all, Carroll. Maybe true love means you're finally just growing up."

"Maybe. You know Heather, I don't think I've ever said no to a woman before."

"So how does it feel, Mister Man?"

"It hurts, but it's a hurt I could learn to live with."

"Well, dammit, if that's how it's going to be, that's how it's going to be. I suppose it's too late for you to get another room, so I get the bed, you get the couch. And don't come kissing around on me if you change your mind."

Chapter 28

Whatever a natural high was, Carroll Thurston had one. He felt a deep, glowing satisfaction he had seldom felt before, partly the result of performing to the best of his ability, and partly because he felt something deep inside himself had changed for the better.

Carroll laughed out loud as he waited by himself for the hotel elevator. It almost didn't seem real, he thought. It just didn't get any better than this.

The bell chimed and the elevator doors whooshed open. Carroll's jaw dropped when he saw that Scud Matthews was on board with a girl wrapped around him who was nibbling on his ear. Carroll recognized her instantly—it was Sugar Shay.

"Well, if it isn't Carroll," she said in her sweet voice. "I wish I had one of those Arm Twisters right about now."

"Don't tell me..." said Carroll, incredulous. "The two of you are..."

"Closer than beans and rice," answered Scud, fully recovered and with a healthy pink glow to his skin. "Don't she look great?"

She did. She wore a low-cut mini dress tight enough to reveal goosebumps.

"She gives great cleavage, man," Scud said proudly.

"She gives great crabs too," said Carroll.

Sugar and Scud both laughed riotously.

"What's the deal with you, man? What was that whole gay thing you had going with Itch?" Carroll asked.

"You know, Carroll, America is the land of opportunity. And I believe in taking advantage of opportunities. If I can move up in the rankings by scaring off a few of the lunkhead fag haters out there, why not? Keep 'em guessing."

"I've got to admit you had me completely fooled," said Carroll.

The elevator stopped at the lobby. They all stepped out.

"You sure you don't want to go for a little sideroom action Itch has worked up? That's where I'll make up my losses and then some. I guarantee you it will be interesting."

"No, thanks anyway."

"Man, you're missing out on the easy money. Should be some really interesting odds, now."

"Yeah, especially since your health has improved overnight."

"That it has. It's a goddamn miracle, ain't it?"

"By the way, I've got a little parting gift for you." Carroll handed him the travelling case with the Thermos bottle.

"Ah, your deluxe roach motel," said Scud. "Gee, thanks."

Carroll gave Sugar Shay a quick kiss on the cheek and said, "Sugar, you are one piece of ass I will never forget. And not just because of the crotch critters either."

"Aw, you're sweet," she said.

"Next time, dude," said Scud.

"Next time it is," said Carroll.

Carroll stopped midway down the hall and turned around. "On second thought, maybe I will see you later. As a spectator of course. Where is it?"

"Madison Room at twelve sharp."

Carroll pointed an imaginary pistol at Scud and pretended to fire it. "Later."

Chapter 29

A few minutes before noon Carroll pushed past the doors of the Madison Room and found himself deep in another world. A chorus of groans greeted him.

"Hell, don't tell me *you're* in on the action today." It was the clearly irked voice of Snack Pack Harris, normally the gentlest of pullers even under the most agonizing pressure.

"Not to worry, big fella," answered Carroll laughingly, "I'm here strictly as a sightseer. I've done my day's work."

"Thank merciful God," said Snack Pack. "I thought you'd shoot my odds all to shit."

A collective sigh of relief went round the large ballroom.

"Mr. Thurston, I presume?" asked a white-haired, slightly stooped old gentleman who walked towards him proudly with the help of a gold-topped cane. He wore a well-cut khaki-colored poplin suit with an old-fashioned string tie.

"I don't believe I've had the pleasure." Carrroll held out his hand.

"I'm Colonel Hermitage T. Halverson. Pleased to make your acquaintance." He grasped Carroll's hand with both of his and shook them vigorously. "I guess you might say I'm in charge of our little get-together here today."

"Colonel Halverson, of course. I've known about you for years and I'm glad to finally meet you. You know it's been over ten years since I paid a visit to one of your 'little get-togethers'."

"Actually, yes I do know. I've been keeping tabs on you since you were first pulling in amateur matches around Memphis." He paused to put a cigarette in a holder and light it. "You are a very impressive man, if I may say so."

"Why thank you."

"I think you may have been bitten by that old celebrity bug," he asked with a twinkle in his eye. "Am I mistaken?"

"No. It's nice to be recognized every once in a while and take home a few extra dollars."

"I never have cared for all that bother," the Colonel said with a dismissive flip of his hand. "The PAWA matches are too tame for my tastebuds. Oh, there's no question about the pulling talent out there. That's not the point. It's just all too predictable and tidy today.

"When I was a young man, you see, my daddy and I ran our plantation together. During the Depression my daddy would pay twenty new silver dollars to the winning puller at the end of our picking and ginning season. Back then around those parts they called it arm-banging. They would take an old wood door and lay it across a couple of sawhorses and that would be the banging table. Folks came from ten counties away, it was held in a big barn, you see. Son, let me tell you, those were the days." The Colonel tapped his cane on the floor for emphasis.

"The hard labor of the times produced some outstanding strong men, and twenty dollars in silver was good money in those days. Almost half a field hand's yearly take, you know. I saw men tie hunting knives to the ends of a table, live yellowjackets, one time even a pair of water moccasins. A fella in the Klan lost one time to a nigra boy up from Alabama, got a double-barrelled shotgun and took that boy's head clean off at the shoulder. Made the worst damned mess you ever saw."

"I can just imagine."

"That's what's missing in all this cleaned-up, fancy pants tournament business. I don't mean to take away from your win or anything, but to me there's just not enough *excitement*. That's why I have my little get-togethers. Pulling wasn't meant to be a clean sport. All this talk about the Olympics. Bah."

Carroll, in fact, had been keenly aware of the Colonel's interest in him since his salad days as a junior puller. There were many not-so-subtle hints and bribes to get him involved in the shadowy side of the sport, but Carroll was following in Steve Strong's proven footsteps and Steve Strong had tried in vain to shut down the sideroom matches. He felt they demeaned the sport, put it on the level of backwater blood-sports like cockfighting.

The Colonel, however, was of the old school. Although he had been called the Colonel his whole adult life—same as his daddy—he didn't have a state commission certifying the honor until he bought one from Tennessee's corrupt Blanton adminis-tration in the seventies. It cost him a thousand dollars in hard cash and the promise of a block of votes in Dunlap County for Governor Blanton's handpicked operators. As one of the biggest and most poweful landowners in West Tennessee, Colonel Halverson had plenty of money for politics and for indulging his passion for arm wrestling.

Like all the sideroom matches fronted by the Colonel, he became the house. All official bets were made through him at odds set by his oddsmakers. A large blackboard was used to post odds and the match-ups. Competitors were allowed to make their own side bets at whatever odds they chose. The Colonel's savvy gaming ensured he seldom lost money. Hundreds of dollars changed hands with every pull.

Unlike the official PAWA tournament, the Colonel used only

three weight classifications: light, medium, and heavy. The winner of each weight class won a flat $10,000. Each participant
paid a thousand-dollar entry fee. The greatest interest, however,
was in the final event, an all-comers match that paid a $30,000
grand prize. Ringers from all over the world were brought in by
high-rolling Vegas gamblers. It was a mean and vicious spectacle
in which wrists were snapped and ligaments shredded with
impunity. Anyone caught fixing or throwing a match or breaking
one of the Colonel's quixotic rules, however, was barred immediately and for life. There was no appeal. The Colonel also held
onto the quaint custom of pullers shaking hands before getting
into position at the table, which they uniformly resented. One
puller who performed a butt-shaking victory strut after whip-
sawing his opponent's arm to the touch pad was banned from all
future events for, according to the Colonel, "bad taste and a
shocking lack of good manners."

As the Colonel and Carroll continued their conversation,
Scud Matthews burst into the room with Sugar Shay on his arm.
They wore matching T-shirts with the inscription I'M WITH
STUPID and little arrows that pointed toward each other.

"Well if it ain't the ole possum hisself," remarked Snack Pack
Harris over a loud murmur among the assembled. "And with a
good-lookin' gal. You turned switcheroo on us?"

"Snack Pack, I'd like you to meet my lovely fiancé, Sugar
Shay," said Scud.

"Naw. Don't tell me you faked us out on the sick fag bit too.
Hell, now I wish your sorry ass did have AIDS," said Snack
Pack Harris bitterly.

"Aw, don't take it so hard, Snack Pack. You never were my
type anyway."

There was a loud rapping of a gavel. As all eyes turned toward
the sound, the Colonel stood alone at a lectern and switched on
a microphone. He tapped the end of the mic to make sure it was
on which caused a deafening squeal of feedback.

"Testing, testing. Is this thing on? Can y'all hear me in the back? Allright then. Ladies and gentlemen, I'd like to take a few moments to welcome you today to the *real* main event, the Colonel Hermitage T. Halverson Arm Wrestling Classic. In case you don't know me, I'm the Colonel. No puller can enter until he is paid up in full. If you haven't paid your entry fee, see Jackie here.

"Most of you know how this event works. The rules call for single-elimination matches, not double-elimination. Ten thousand for the winner of each weight class. Thirty thousand to the winner of the final event." He chuckled. "I want to assure you we have a surprise or two in store, so be sure to stick around to the end.

"Without further ado, we'll let the games begin after Reverend Ellington leads us in a word of prayer. I do hope you all are up to date on your medical insurance."

Carroll watched with great interest as familiar pullers went arm-to-arm with powerful men he had never seen before. Although there was a referee, enforcement of typical tournament rules was lax. Pullers were allowed to break their grips at will, which excited the bettors, but to a professional like Carroll made the game dull as dirt. Because many of the entrants were strong but unproven, there were more prolonged power struggles at the table which resulted in a far greater number of injuries. Few of the ringers were a match for the solid pros, but the few who were cleaned up at the betting table.

Scud and Itch's elaborate deceptions finally made sense to Carroll. By pretending to be sick with AIDS, Itch was able to place side bets well in advance at odds that paid much more handsomely. The odds changed instantly when Scud turned up rosy-cheeked and heterosexual.

In the heavyweight class Scud Matthews had beaten everyone

except Snack Pack Harris, who stopped him dead with a quick holding maneuver and dragged him down to the touch pad using his massive body weight. Carroll thought to himself that Scud didn't put up much of a fight. He wondered if Scud and Itch weren't simply manipulating the odds for the main event. "Probably," he concluded to himself.

As the Colonel was overseeing a table wipe-down for the final event, an enormous hulk of a man walked into the room with two bodyguards at his side. The man stood six-foot flat, but had on platform shoes with heels that boosted his height at least another three inches. Carroll was an expert judge of puller flesh and could tell right off the bat this guy would be a killer at the Jeffrey table. Even heavily muscled arms often had too much length and lank, making their pulling angles awkward and inefficient. If the shoulder-to-elbow contour wasn't just so or the slope from forearm to wrist leveled off at the wrong point, all the muscle in the world couldn't correct the genetic flaw of improper proportion. This guy's proportions were like something out of a *Gray's Anatomy*. His right arm was textbook-perfect. Carroll noticed the man's slight swayback and a prominently protruding gut. It was the hugely pumped thighs that gave him away. He had to be a power lifter.

Itch whispered to Scud, "It's a guy named Larry Lancaster from San Diego. A power lifter. No doubt about it, he's got power."

"Why are the meatballs with him?"

"He's one of the mob's boy toys. They don't want anyone fucking with him."

One look at Larry Lancaster and the oddsmakers reacted as if they were caught in a flurry at the New York Stock Exchange. Lancaster was called on deck for the first match-up with a middleweight from Greece who had more balls than brains. The odds were ridiculously lopsided in Lancaster's favor. Lancaster easily stopped the puller in mid-move and audibly gritted his teeth as he applied a downward wrenching pressure. The puller's face twisted in agony as everyone heard a loud crack and a long slice of bone knifed through the side of his wrist. He fainted before he could scream.

Scud and Snack Pack similarly had been mismatched with lighter weight pullers foolhardy enough to think they had a winning chance. Nearly every one of the smaller men walked away, or was carried away, with injuries and empty pockets, much to the delight of Colonel Halverson.

"Larry Lancaster and Snack Pack Harris, on deck."

As the two pullers dusted up at the rosin bowl, the Colonel approached the lectern.

"Ladies and gentlemen. As you know, the final all-comers match is the single most demanding event in the sport of pulling. Also, since I put up the prize money, I call the shots. In many past events we have done various things to spice up the action. We're down now to the final three contestants and we're going to try something new and a little different. Could someone please turn down the house lights?"

As the lights were dimmed, the Colonel placed a small metal canister at the end of the Jeffrey table. He opened a valve and the canister gave off a mild hiss. He held a striker to the canister's nozzle and the shower of sparks it produced gave way with a "fwoosh!" to a steady orange flame. He put another of the canisters at the table's opposite end and lit it.

Stepping back to the lectern, he leaned in to the microphone. "Two propane tanks are being used as our touch pad targets, folks. I don't think we'll see any serious injury from it, but it should make things a sight more interesting."

"Christ, what a sick little bastard," Carroll thought to himself.

As Snack Pack Harris and Larry Lancaster shook their hands and put their elbows into their cups, Snack Pack couldn't take his eyes off the flame. His brow was deeply ridged and he looked more anxious than Carroll had ever remembered seeing him.

174   Tom Graves

When the go was given, Snack Pack hesitated and was immediately overwhelmed by Larry Lancaster, who again gritted his
teeth so loudly they could be heard by the roomful of spectators.
It was now a power showdown and Snack Pack had a late start
and poor concentration. Lancaster had angled Snack Pack
towards the touch pad before he could properly muster his great
strength. Snack Pack was driven closer and closer to the table
until the propane flame licked the hairs on his arm where they
promptly ignited and flared like the filaments in a thousand tiny
lightbulbs.

Snack Pack howled in pain and jerked his arm back from the
table. The Colonel laughed until he was convulsed in a hacking
smoker's cough. One of the Colonel's assistants brought a tube
of unguent to Snack Pack, who quickly applied it to his burn,
which was beginning to blister.

"Testing, testing," said the Colonel as the microphone began
to squeal again. "We're down to the showdown match of the
afternoon between Mr. Scud Matthews and Mr. Larry Lancaster.
You can see the odds posted. May the better man win."

Scud and Lancaster shook hands warily and bent together
into their grip. Scud seemed unusually serious and subdued. As
the go was given, Scud blasted forward with his wrist slightly
bowing his opponent's. Lancaster, however, with his tremendous power hung in tight, scarcely budging. They squared off
with their faces turning redder by the split second, the table
vibrating from the tension and strain of the pullers' muscles.
Scud allowed his wrist to break backwards in a sudden, snapping motion, a move designed to give Lancaster a false sense of
gaining ground. At the same time Scud drove forward with the
heel of his palm and began his trademark snaking wrist twists.
Lancaster, losing arm balance, began to buckle. As his arm was
catapulted towards the burner flame, he did the unthinkable.
With his free hand he grabbed Scud's wrestling arm, pulling
against Scud with both arms instead of one. Scud's arm lunged

towards the flame and he rocketed his left hand hard into Lancaster's chin. Lancaster stopped a fraction away from the burner and nose-dived into the table.

Out of the corner of his eye, Carroll saw one of the bodyguards reach into his sport jacket. Taking a running jump, Carroll brought the guard down savagely with a flying kick. A chrome-plated revolver broke free of the guard's hand and skidded across the ballroom floor.

As the remaining bodyguard reflexively reached for his pistol, he felt a cold barrel nudge his scrotum from behind and heard a loud click.

"Want to keep 'em?" Itch half-whispered in his ear.

"Yeah," the bodyguard answered.

"Then take your hand away from that piece or you'll get the world's fastest vasectomy."

Chapter 30

A s the taxi pulled into Pamela's driveway, the front door flew open and Byron and Pamela raced to meet him. They both smothered Carroll in a flurry of hugs and kisses.

Carroll handed Byron his large trophy. "I won the PAWA Tournament," he said.

"We know," Pamela said as she hugged Carroll again tightly.

"We know," Byron repeated, giddy with the excitement.

"We called the tournament officials and they told us everything," she smiled. "They even told us you had booked a flight to Nashville. So we've been expecting you. I hope you're hungry. Supper's waiting."

"I'm always hungry for your cooking, sweetheart," Carroll said.

When they finished eating, Carroll said, "Pammy, there are a few people I need to call and tell about my win. Would you mind?"

"Heather and Barry?" she asked.

"Actually, just Barry and my folks."

"Sure, go ahead. The bedroom phone will give you a little privacy."

Pamela was clearing off the table when Carroll came back. He slid his massive arms around her tiny waist and kissed her warmly.

"God, I love you," he said.

"And I love you," she said without cracking a smile.

"Why don't you run off with Byron for awhile while I finish up."

"Sure you don't need some help here in the kitchen?"

"I'm sure. Go ahead."

Carroll joined Byron in the den and asked him if it wasn't a very special occasion.

"Uh-huh, today is a vewy special occasion. You won and bwought the twophy."

"Let's treat ourselves then, whattya say?"

"Okay."

Carroll rifled through the video cabinet and found what he was looking for. He put the tape in the VCR and pressed the play button and he settled back into the sofa next to Byron.

Geraldo Rivera was talking to a group of skinheads when a civil rights activist began to choke a young white supremacist. The *Geraldo* set erupted in chaos and violence as fists and chairs flew across the stage.

The next scene cut to Geraldo with a swollen, bloody nose speaking with great solemnity into the camera.

Byron began to snicker and Carroll joined in until they both were laughing, laughing their asses off.

THE END

Acknowledgments

Although *Pullers* is a product of my warped imagination, I owe a debt of thanks to many friends and colleagues who lent moral support, encouragement, and on more than one occasion a shoulder to whine on. Phil Jones, Cathy Dice, John Knepper, John Stafford, Robert Propst, Madeleine Morel, and my lovely sister-in-law, Diane Scott, were all early and enthusiastic readers who provided clear-eyed feedback and suggestions. Gerald Beatty and Terry Jacobus, two world-class athletes, gave me invaluable insider's knowledge into their respective sports. Al Virelli and The New Orleans Historic Voodoo Museum, likewise, provided information no one else could. A tip of the hat to my mother also, for always being there for me. Jim Newcomb, who was and remains my teacher, I owe more than words can express. A special thanks also to my Bennington Writers Workshop posse (1996) and to Barney Rosset, Gabriel Morgan, Henno Lohmeyer, and Peter Leers who believed in *Pullers* enough to publish it. I can't end this without acknowledging three writers who greatly influenced me and this work: my old pal John Fergus Ryan, the late Charles Willeford, and Harry Crews. Read them.